ORO CITY

D.E. VINCENT

outskirts press

Oro City

v1.0

This is a work of fiction. Names, characters, businesses, places, events, locales, and incidents are either the products of the author's imagination or used in a fictitious manner. Any resemblance to actual persons, living or dead, or actual events is purely coincidental.

The opinions expressed in this manuscript are solely the opinions of the author and do not represent the opinions or thoughts of the publisher. The author has represented and warranted full ownership and/or legal right to publish all the materials in this book.

Outskirts Press, Inc.
http://www.outskirtspress.com

Paperback ISBN: 978-1-9772-4309-6

PRINTED IN THE UNITED STATES OF AMERICA

ORO CITY

I've decided to write all this down so that one day you will know what it was truly like living in such an inhospitable, albeit gloriously beautiful, place. I also want to tell the story of some of those who ventured there and how their presence gave merit and distinction to a tiny Colorado mountain town, Oro City.

To begin the adventures of Jasper Gratz as he is central to this telling I will start back in the Old Country. A brief physical description of the boy would include: gray eyes, nut brown hair and a face sprinkled with freckles. Right under and to the side of his left eye was a distinctive strawberry colored birthmark. Heart shaped and the size of a small fingernail. This mark was easily overlooked once Jasper opened his mouth and spoke. He was good natured and curious about the world around him, and was a strapping lad of fourteen when tales of the new west in America began appearing in the German village of Aachen where his family had lived for generations. The stories were fantastical to him in every way.

Jasper had a vivid imagination which served him well as he worked side by side with his older brother Horst at the blacksmith shop. One day the smithy Bakke, to whom they were both apprenticed, received a letter from a relative who had immigrated to America in 1863. The letter was shared and circulated throughout the village for days before the brothers chanced to hear of it. He and Horst knew how to read from days spent choring for the parson after each service - when the parson took time to school them. And too, the parson required that the boys follow the readings during services. So sitting down outside the shop while taking a break, Horst and Jasper read the letter.

The Letter

Bakke's cousins had traveled by wagon to the edge of the Rocky Mountains from a Missouri outpost, a long and arduous trip of 22 months. Eventually they came to a hustle bustle confluence of two modest rivers. Some called the makeshift settlement Auraria. It was a stopping off place to pick up supplies and implements if one was of a mind to journey to the gold strikes of Gregory Gulch or Blackhawk. The cousins didn't describe much about the place in the letter Horst read to Jasper, other than that the late spring mud was particularly thick and foul-smelling with animal dung and the place thick with flies. Not very appealing.

Also, read the letter, one of the cousins, Samuel, had contracted a mild case of influenza and was directed to a tent where a generous spirited woman named Augusta Tabor wrapped his neck and chest with a healing poultice. Having been spared a serious illness, it was only a week or so later that Sam and his brother, Peter, were able to resume their trek into the foothills in hopes of good fortune. The young man, Samuel, will be reminded of this good woman's skills later in this narrative.

Meanwhile, in Aachen Jasper was quite taken with imagining what all the places in this letter of Bakke's must be like. In fact he determined to do everything that he could to get to the western parts of America himself, and soon as possible. Jasper's parents had no money to spare, having five more children younger than himself; but the smithy Bakke made a contribution which created the probability within three years for his passage on a steam ship. He would miss his family, but most of all brother Horst with whom he had spent a great deal of his youth. Everyone wished him a prosperous future. His dear mother kissed him through her streaming tears. She did not think she would see her son again this side of paradise.

To America

The ocean crossing had Jasper working as a fireman in the bowels of a steamer shoveling coal into the blazing furnaces. He was young and strong. And determined. The work was neither hardship nor imposition, and more importantly aided him with the cost of his passage. As he would discover with passing time his apprenticeship as a smithy would continue serving him well as he journeyed forth into the unknown.

He disembarked in New York harbor, but first had to go through a confusing time on Ellis Island. While waiting his turn to be processed Jasper shared a bench with a fellow who had the letters TONY drawn on his forehead with sooty coal chalk. Being curious he asked what the letters meant, but was answered in Italian, which he didn't understand. Another from Germany told him that once a man left the ship which had brought him across the ocean, officials on the island used this method to direct authorities to which mainland port the person should be sent; therefore, "to New York" was common to see on many a brow. And it was for this reason that so many men ended up in the New World with the first name of Tony.

Along this same vein most immigrants with long ancestral surnames found that officials would chop off many letters and leave people with shortened easier to pronounce names. Jasper was thankful that Gratz was spelled simple to begin with and as such was left intact. Thankful also because a surname tethered one to his native place.

I, Jasper, Venture Westward

Many remarkable adventures accompanied me as I traveled the eastern part of this wondrous land. In fact many numerous and opportune happenings fueled my resolve to see my dream through to the end, which I heartily hoped was the Colorado Territory. My journey began on a flatboat navigating the Ohio River which afforded me a sense of the bountiful nature of the continent. Having to be ferried across the Mississippi underscored my high adventures. Numerous wagons were being outfitted for the western crossing and once my trade as a blacksmith had been noted folks were eager to have me join their wagon train. My knowhow made me a boon. And it wasn't long before joining a train that I proved my worth by keeping horses shod and wagon wheels in good repair. As always I took my share of teasing about my heart-shaped birthmark while never taking offense. No matter, for all I knew the mark would fade in time.

One woeful incident occurred after I had fashioned a wedding band for a grateful young couple, Tobias and Lucinda Poole. I was asked to use a cast off broach once worn, I was told, by a disgruntled matron with a soiled past. Be this as it may, no one questioned how the ornament found its way into the possession of the bride to be, and regardless, the final product was quite handsome. The two were married by the wagon master. Lucinda, a winsome lass with black hair that wisped in soft curls about her dimpled cheeks, had a remarkable singing voice which she used to provide all the folks with entertainment on many evenings, the choicest song on her wedding night. And it was with this delightful selection "Green Grow the Lilacs" that I found myself quite bedazzled.

Heartbreaking anguish came about when Tobias was bitten by a timber rattler while hunting rabbits near a wooded hillside a day and a half out of St. Joe. Because he wasn't complaining loudly of the bites, he did succumb to the venom within a few hours' time. His bride, tears streaming from her green eyes, was in a state of delirium and so the train's good doctor supplied her with a substantial quantity of laudanum. More than once this drug was to be the dulcet Lucinda's near undoing. However, when I again encountered her in the gold fields a long time hence she appeared to be no longer under its influence.

There is no chance of shortening this tale by bypassing details of the months which had been drawn out nearly two years crossing rivers, grasslands and barren plains.

Most people traveling west by any manner of conveyance were terrified by stories of marauding Indians. I will only say that my wagon train was spared terrorizing visits by native tribes. As it happened, of the native peoples which we encountered most were as curious about us as we were of them. And on a few occasions we were favorably surprised by offers of simple trades.

One day for instance, our journey took us quite near a handsome village of some dozen mud and rock structures. Three men dressed in native attire and looking anything but fierce approached just as dusk was coming on. We'd been setting up for the night and had already built small cook fires, when the trio demonstrated a wish to join us. We parlayed for a short time, each party making use of hand gestures and facial expressions, until a mutual agreement was reached. We accepted two handsome buffalo robes - the natives, half a barrel of coarse cornmeal, which they poured into leather satchels, and a small sack of sugar. All were of a mind that the exchange was fair. The locals rode off northward to their village leaving behind quite a favorable impression.

The previous spring we had a heart stopping occurrence while being ferried across the mighty Missouri River. Mrs. Wagner and her month old infant were in the seventh wagon in line to cross. Generally people stood beside the river and watched as each wagon was floated across, and as such we were all witnesses to the event. When the ropes securing it broke loose from the ferry boat, the wagon bed drifted into the swirling current. Mother and child went whirling downstream. But quite miraculously two horsemen rode into the river and were able to grab the ropes and tie them to their saddle horns as the wagon floated by. Back on the riverbank a few men on horseback were straining mightily to hold on. Soon thereafter a dozen men rushed to their aid and the wagon was pulled to safety.

As with incidents great or small in consequence, folks carried on with the day's duties and very little time was spent sympathizing with hapless victims. Mrs. Wagner was observed that same evening rocking her babe after preparing a possum stew for the family supper.

Our journey had lumbered on for six endless months and as autumn was fast drawing to an end the train decided to winter in a rather primitive place. Fort Hays had been erected by the

U.S. army several months before as the nation was in the grips of civil war. I had a vague recollection of a similar outpost that Bakke's cousins had spoken of in their long ago letter home to my German village, Aachen. I found myself longing more and more frequently to be on my own so as to travel more speedily, but my fellow emigrants counseled me to remain in this place until spring. As I deliberated long and hard, the isolation of the barren landscape eventually aided me in a decision to stay with the train.

The winter was coming on cold and somewhat harsh with sleet and rain. Just the week before we were caught in a thunderstorm lashing us with rain and pelting us with hail. It fell to the heavily overworked women to unload wagons after a downpour so damp goods could be dried out. These brave females also pitched the tents and saw to the yoking of the oxen. If you were of the gentle sex labor never ended. Nevertheless late evenings were often filled with folk songs from various homelands. And Lucinda Poole, her wide shimmery green eyes reflecting a yearning hopefulness, continued to delight all with heartfelt musical renditions. That is, if she were feeling robust enough.

After this latest storm we built lean-tos to hold the weather from the north at bay, but truthfully even with buffalo robes tacked on, these shelters were of little practical use. Our wagons were in a circular formation and large fires in the center area attempted to allow for some sense of safety and warmth. The wagons often had to be staked down because of high winds. Daylight hours found me plenty busy making numerous repairs on the wagons. And too, visits with many of the folks afforded me good reason to sustain a light-hearted mood.

More and more I realized that when I visualized scenery I

did such in German and when I dreamed I did so in German. My German language afforded me a vastly larger vocabulary, more descriptors.

Even so, I determined to practice the English language along with my blacksmith work, so as to make the long days pass in an industrious manner. I entreated a genial fellow name of Charlie Hennessy to tutor me. He was well versed in The Good Book and used it to teach me the alphabet. He was a strict taskmaster who had once held a teaching position, and saw to it that I practiced for some hours each day. At times I found him quite wearisome with his frequent teasing about my small red birthmark. Nonetheless, in a few months' time I could read simple sentences aloud. I took to the language easily and whiled away hours attempting to converse with any sap who was dipping a pail at the Fort's well where I would generally linger.

Folks remarked that I used a common man's parlance which made sense considering my teacher, who'd had merely a spattering of formal schooling, Charlie was none too refined and thinking back I can't recall ever seeing him without a plug of chewin' tobacco in his cheek, and a stream of juice spat out. And so it followed that it was my English language teacher who gifted me with this crude habit.

Christmas was a notable time because of the variety of customs which people had brought with them from their homelands. In spite of the bleakness of the wintery landscape the camp's mood was festive rather than homesick-choked. Plenty of that but instead of longing for what we had left behind we seemed determined to be happy and hopeful about what lay before us. Singing songs and describing foods from so many foreign places helped all to forge a bond of unity rather than to underscore diversity. We were one and the same in our desire for a better life which allowed the peace of the season to embrace our communal heart.

As for myself, the memories of this particular Christmas will remain inscribed with fondness in my heart forever, for as the pretty Lucinda sang for us she seemed to focus her gaze in my direction. I felt that she would see the longing in my heart.

Spring came eventually as we knew it would. We started out after the rains gentled but alas encountered miseries unlike any we had faced before. First, clouds of insects had to be driven off with smudges. And also grease buckets, the grease made with animal fats and tar, swung from each wagon's rear axle. The ongoing spreading of grease on the wheels was a necessary burden of every traveler.

And mud. The wagon wheels were clogged with it and constantly had to be scraped using stout sticks, the same implement used for greasing. Days on end found the lot of us slogging through six inches deep of the dreadful muck. All but the very young and the mothers near their laying-in time walked beside the wagons. Many appreciated that the soil when dry would be a rich dark brown, albeit stony, but likely good for farming; however for now the oxen, mules, and humans mutely endured the miserable trail. Of some mention, the plains had been treeless for hundreds of miles. Common practice was to gather dried buffalo dung to use as fuel. All were expected to collect the stuff as we walked along, but the women bore the brunt. In spite of all these difficulties dreams of a new and better life filled each and every head, and it was these visions alone that kept all of us plodding westward.

Into the Mountains

For almost two weeks every eye had been drawn to the incredibly majestic peaks of the Shining Mountains, now called the Rockies. Someone thought that a really high one was called Pike's Peak. Another man said we were too far north for a sighting of Pike's Peak. The horizon was an absolute wonderment and so timely that our imaginations were unleashed and the permeating mood was jubilation. At long last we arrived at the base of the foothills and sighted the struggling settlement of Auraria, and too the mushrooming town of Denver City a few miles to the northeast. The soft warm days of early spring greeted us and all who had been my companions for the last several months congratulated one another for sticking with it through thick and thin. The majority of the wagons were going on toward California and Oregon. But this would be my stopping off place.

My clothes needed washing as did my body. I spotted a makeshift structure affording some privacy, paid for a warmish tub of water and scrubbed my body with a hard brick of soap that was provided. I then handed coins to a woman to wash my clothes but she pronounced that they were in tatters and hardly worthwhile. No surprise since I had been unable to change any of these items since leaving home. Therefore, I would have to make do with the same ragged shirt and trousers until I could purchase new ones.

A Player Named Pepper

Next I set about trying to acquire a burro, the Spanish name for jackass. Many a bewhiskered old cuss who'd spent years prospecting suggested that burros were lovable pack animals. They were smallish, just this side larger than a goat, and assured to be an agreeable companion in most situations. I found a corral amidst a cottonwood grove holding an assortment of four legged animals. So now I approached a group of scraggly looking young men who were draped over the fence. Each studied me languidly which made me conscious of my foreignness, but regardless I resolved to buy a burro with wages earned from wagon repairs. I took an hour to inspect several offerings and after some earnest deliberations settled on a tannish colored animal with hind quarters sprinkled with many black spots. His fur coloring reminded me of pepper, so that's what his name would be. As I handed over money for his purchase Pepper turned in my direction and brayed quite disagreeably.

My next task was to purchase needed supplies with nearly the last of my wages. Clothes: a fur cap, thick scarf, extra flannel shirts, canvas trousers, red long johns, heavy coat and high lace-up boots. I took time to exchange my rags for the new britches and one of the shirts. Cooking: frying pan, coffee pot, and matches. Food: lard, flour, dried beans, coffee, and salt. Extras: tobacco, candles, hatchet, length of rope, bowie knife, and Sharps rifle. All of these items were secured to a wooden cross-saddle fitted onto my new burro's back; there was a canvas sling which was cinched under his belly to hold the contraption in place. I fashioned a rucksack out of canvas to be worn by myself so as not to over-burden my burro, a consideration which the animal would prove to be wholly undeserved. An eight foot length of rope was to be used as a lead. And I now felt ready as I could manage and as well-equipped as possible for whatever might lay ahead.

My 19th birthday was spent leading my burro Pepper along a trail while climbing steadily. Four days out of Denver City, I'd been thinking of camping by a small stream in the middle of a wide valley known as South Park. When I happened upon a wizened prospector he agreeably shared his fire ring. I tied Pepper to a nearby tree next to a dun colored mule. Then sat and inquired of the fellow where he had last been prospecting.

"I've been over to a gold camp called Oro City. Spent some time on my placer claim, but the gold is most played out in all of California Gulch. A lode gold mine named Printer Boy was just beginning operations but I was mostly played out myself. So I stuffed my pouch of gold dust into a well-hidden pocket and left the place."

The prospector went on for some time schooling me on the workings of placer gold mining. From time immemorial gold had washed into streams and creeks from high peaks. The gold settled in the creek beds. All a man had to do was pan for the treasure. Later on a wooden sluice box placed across the stream was the method of working a claim. This was called placer mining.

We passed a pleasant evening talking of the gold fields here and about. But I wanted to know more about Oro City. Gold or no gold.

"How would someone such as myself find a route into the high mountains with a final stopping-off place being this California Gulch?"

"Keep on following the South Platte and you'll come to a mining camp name of Alma. Go along a stream they call Mosquito, same name as the pass. You'll be climbing steadily in a northwest direction. Be looking for a trail, but trail or no just climb until you can't no more. By and by you'll get to Oro City on the other side of this same pass."

A chilly night followed. Then before the next morning got warm darned if the old guy didn't insist I take his animal as my own. He said that whenever I found some color, meaning gold, I could come on back and pay him, and that I'd find him someplace nearby like as not.

"Why would you want to be free of such a personal possession?"

"The mule is of no consequence to me as I'm quit of this way of life. I'm going back to Denver City and an easier life. After fifteen years I am plumb wore out as I already mentioned."

"Well, I thank you for the gift and all the useful information. And good luck to you from here on out."

His offer seemed good fortune as mules were choice for packing and Pepper would likely not mind a mate.

Well, Pepper did mind. And he put on quite a show to convince me to reconsider this unwelcome chum. He yanked his head and pulled loose of the rope, and proceeded to wedge himself between two spruces so as to scrape the pack from his back. I nearly swallowed my chew when he bellowed in outrage, a sound extremely harsh and baleful as any I'd ever heard.

When I had gingerly repacked his load and retied the rope tightly to a tree, I looked him squarely in the eye and implored him to behave. His response was to calmly chomp on some nearby grasses.

I took the gift-mule back to the old guy and shook my head emphatically.

"Nope. Can't take him off your hands."

I made camp that night along with my high-minded burro in the neighborhood of Alma, where an assayer name of Begler had hung his sign in plain sight. I made a mental note to remember where in case a need of the man's knowledge ever came my way.

It was quiet and the night was gentle as again I found myself beside a tributary of the South Platte River. It was always favorable to camp next to water. Too frigid for bathing but good for washing up and even soaking tired feet. I fashioned a bed by laying soft pine boughs down and topping them with a blanket. My customary pillow was a bundle of clothes. I had no complaints. And after checking on Pepper's present disposition, he actually gave forth a contented sigh. So now I determined to sleep soundly beside my campfire.

Pepper and me set off with the rising sun not even taking time to boil a pot of coffee. Anyways around mid- afternoon I was feeling right grown up and independent at age nineteen. It was then that I found myself in the company of a freight wagon ever since crossing a bitty fork at the headwaters of the South Platte. Earlier I'd been a good piece ahead of the wagon, but every now and then I had to stop and settle differences with Pepper. Seemed that a little too often we had a contest to see who was truly boss of the outfit. No doubt we both knew who took the prize as the most contrary of the pair.

Also, just lately I'd decided to take time to try my luck at catching a fish for my dinner. Finally I gave it up realizing that I lacked proper know-how for such an enterprise. Same lack of luck with capturing small game.

So now the driver was once again up ahead and me coughing dust from wagon wheels while gnawing on yet another piece of pemmican. Now that's a story right there:

Some days back I needed meat and came across five fellows of the Ute tribe. Well I found them willing to trade a small billows I'd carried all the way from Bakke's blacksmith shop. They showed me a sizable pouch of a dried meat substance, pemmican, and then by use of gestures assured me that unlike fresh meat, pemmican would not go bad. But before the exchange could be made I in turn had to demonstrate how a billows would make a hard-to-start fire flare up real fast and good. We parted ways friendly, but as this tough pasty concoction wasn't any too tasty, it's a question who got the better trade.

By and by the wagon loaded down with tenting materials, picks, shovels, double jacks and crates of root vegetables was again directly in my way. So, just as I started pulling Pepper around it, the wagon driver suddenly rolled a wheel into a narrow ditch and the load tipped precariously toward a steep embankment.

"Hey, boy! Give a hand!"

I dropped Pepper's rope. "Where you want me to hold onto?"

"Get on the down side and put your shoulder to it. I'll say when to shove."

Groaning deep in my guts and digging both boots into some rocky soil I gave it my all. This was not of much use because right then the wagon tipped in earnest and I quick had to jump up slope out of its way.

The driver leaped from his perch with no little time to think. And then the two of us watched as the wagon rolled and the goods spilled out onto the stony earth. Driver cussed a stream 'fore all was settled. And now he had a taxing job of rescuing his mule to boot. Nothing much that I could see to do after all this happening so I took my leave of the messy aftermath.

Once more me and old Pepper set off up the trail; the two of us seemed to have a meeting of the minds for now. After a time of me sweating and drawing in deep drafts of thin air we rounded a small escarpment. Halting right there I tipped my head back squinting and gazing and then gasping.

The sight was fearsome as any I'd seen on a trip full of fearsomeness. The trail ahead was steep and twisting and full of every kind of obstacle as far and beyond as I could see. The burro and I had left forests behind an hour before, and now all was giant rocks and lots of gravelly stones rolling under my boots, such as to trip me unawares. Banks of snowfields up above also left me dumbfounded and scratching my head. Pepper was in his element, unfazed.

"Boy!"

My head whipped around and darned if it wasn't the driver leading his mule still in harnesses and dragging a load of wares from the overturned wagon. He had used some of the tenting as a sledge of sorts to pile on a crate of vegetables and some shovels, picks, and a double-jack hammer.

I waited for him to draw near before returning his greeting.

"Name's Jasper Gratz. How you think to manage that load on this track anyways?"

"I'll do it or die trying! Name's Otis A. Walls, but go ahead and call me Otis."

"And luck to you, Otis. I'll give a hand if it comes to it."

"Be much obliged, Jasper. And that be the god's truth."

After this brief exchange I tugged on Pepper's rope and we commenced climbing. Before long it was more like scrambling using hands and feet to gain purchase of that trail. Me and Pepper changed places so that now he was in front pulling me and having no trouble keeping his balance. The sun's glare was causing me to squint under my floppy hat as I tried to skirt the larger of the snowbanks.

Whenever I looked back Otis was struggling mightily with his mule. I held up, my breathing labored. After some minutes of resting, the distance between us closed so I could ask a question without hollering. I took note of the fact that Otis had chucked the vegetable crate off the load.

"You climbed this trail before, Otis?"

"Yes sir, I have. People the other side and on down call the pass Mosquito. It is most treacherous but still folks give her a try regardless of difficulty. They got stars in their eyes and gold in their dreams even though the gold is most played out over in California Gulch. Might be the first and last time I try her with a wagon, yep."

"I heard about the played-out gold fields from an old cuss a day or two ago. But how about you?" I said. "You a prospector?" I figured him to be my brother Horst's age, 24 years or so.

Pulling out a rag he wiped sweat from his brow and neck. He was a well-set- up person - dark and swarthy complexion and sporting an admirable beard and mustache. As for my own whiskers, just a shadow so far.

"Was about a year ago. Did my fair share of working a claim, but then shacks and cabins was building up around the hills and I had a notion to turn my interests to hauling freight for the store-keeps because the pay was up to five cents a pound. I hauled loads two different times through summer and fall by way of Granite. But after this day I've a mind to shuck it all and head back eastward to my people in Ohio."

I nodded my interest. Although the beauty of the hills and gorges kept me awestruck.

"Along with these reasons to quit the mountains, Jasper, I heard a story about some bandits here about." He drew in deep drafts of air before continuing. "They were the notorious Reynolds gang who waited for the Buckskin Joe coach which would be carrying thousands of dollars of gold dust from the mines. As the coach came down the road the gang of robbers swarmed in and stole the gold bags, shot the driver and guard, then burned the conveyance.

"Here's the strange part. Later after most of the outlaws had all been captured, one of the Reynolds brothers dying of a gunshot wound claimed that he'd buried some gold bags in the mountains. He even had a map which told with drawings to go along Geneva Creek up to the head of a gulch, turn right, follow the mountain around a little further to the headwaters of Deer Creek at timberline. But after many, many attempts to recover the treasure no one could find it.

"So they say it's still out here somewheres. And one or two of the gang are still at large to this day."

"So you're scared of robbers and want to throw in the towel, but don't you have an interest in finding the lost treasure before you actually get around to quitting?"

"Yep. I guess so. But not too big an interest."

We had been sitting beside a creek and filling two canteens apiece. Our animals slurping and slurping. The sun was going fast on our side of the pass and was quickly turning into shadows. Clouds were amassing. I could actually taste rain.

"Might we be figuring out some kind of shelter to share for the night, Otis?"

Well this notion got him considering and studying his load.

"What we could do is stretch some of this tenting across those two boulders up yonder and pile the goods underneath next to us. This might keep us out of the weather any rate." And he added, "I held back some taters from the load. Whenever we have time to make a fire they'll be mighty tasty roasted."

As he set about making camp he said, "You should hobble your burro while there's still enough light to see by."

This last bit was welcome advice, me being new to animal ownership. But first, he had to show me how to fashion a hobble-rope. I'll tell how later.

I was able with Otis' help to push over a dead stump and a fire was easily started, so we ate roasted taters that night after all. Otis thought them were all we had, and I managed to keep my mouth shut.

Morning came. My teeth were chattering as I was freezing cold from an uncomfortable night of blowing wind and spitting snow. Being stiff and sore I was sure anxious to get moving again. I shared some pemmican with Otis but my store was steadily dwindling.

"Think our animals would like a sample of this here pemmican?"

"Won't eat meat. Only what they graze on. They'll go a long while yet, no need to find feed for them. Once we top this pass and start down the other side they'll forage on their own."

This was good information. I keep finding myself being schooled as I go along. Ol' Pepper will let me know when I make a mistake, no doubt about that at all.

Otis pulled hard tack from his shirt pockets to share. I didn't think these rock hard biscuits were any more appetizing than my fare. However, next he pulled out a flask of whisky and tipped it down his throat then handed it over to me.

Matter of fact I'd seen plenty of fellows drink the stuff all along the wagon trail but I was never so curious as to try it out myself. Now though, I took a sip hoping to abate the misery in every part of my body. I felt heat all the way down to my boots. Welcome surprise. Whisky took the snap right out of my hush-hush complaining.

"I carry a small-sized coffee bean grinder in my pack. Comes in handy. Coffee sure would hit the spot. Too bad the root vegetables had to be shed as the crates could have served as kindling. Say. Mind me asking what that strawberry heart's doing under your eye? Looks like jam. "

"Born with it, is all. Used to be a lot darker. Seems to be fading."

This is the moment when I sheepishly let him know that I'd stuffed a half dozen potatoes into my pack after the wreck. He seemed thoroughly delighted to have the option of additional taters. So no harm done.

Thinking about coffee, Otis said, "Guess we're lucky just to have water in our canteens. No time for such musings as we've got better part of a day 'fore we even get near to clearing this ridge. From Fairplay to summit is 15 miles, they say."

We packed up the tenting and the few tools Otis had been

able to salvage from the wrecked wagon. And then we had to refigure a harness to strap onto the mule. It was quite an unwieldy contraption, but the mule seemed game so once more we started out on the upslope. Also, Pepper seemed to be agreeable to being tied onto the rope again, me leading.

Just about then some kind of critter that Otis called a marmot started up fussing nearby. Looked to me to be a smallish beaver-like creature tailless with chocolate fur. Wouldn't be the last strange animal citing I'd see the day. But as fast as that thought struck, Pepper bolted and tore back down the slope we'd just climbed.

I didn't know enough cuss words in English so I shouted them out in German. I don't think I ever in my life felt such fury and frustration as I did at that moment. Down I ran fast as I could giving chase. I almost took a tumble into a snow field. Finally within fifteen minutes or so I spied the devil lingering by some bushy brush and nibbling without a care in the world. He paid me no heed as I stomped on down to him.

"If I ever have a juicy apple or carrot in my possession, I will not be sharing it with the likes of you. Just bear that in mind, you demon. Now get moving!"

Time we caught back up with Otis again he was taking a timeout sitting on a mossy rock. One look at me and he set to cackling.

"Trouble with burros is they take a notion to do something and there's just no arguing them out of it."

"Humph. Glad I could serve you up some merriment, Otis. Next time the joke might just be on you."

"Why say you such as that?"

"Cause watching you gnaw on that hard tack doesn't take much imagining to see a tooth or two falling out into your lap."

"Ah ha. So it seems I've met my match in trading witticisms!"

Onwards and upwards we labored. It was tough going for hours and hours. The weather was holding fair and calm which was a good omen, but I thought to myself that hard as my travels had thus far been, nothing could hold a candle to attempting to conquer a mountain slope such as this. The gravel was challenging as I worked my feet across the switch-back inclines. Leg muscles I never knew I had were burning.

Then suddenly I lost my footing and fell scraping my shin on sharp rocks. Pepper had been pulling me along but now stopped and turned to give me one of his looks. He seemed to jerk his chin at me. "Oh, what have I gotten myself into with this burro?" I said under my breath.

Otis seemed to be faring quite well and in fact had been whistling a melody for the better part of an hour. He preferred one toon in particular. We stopped to take a breather.

"That's a catchy song, Otis. What's it called anyways?"

"Why me mam always had us singing "Ol' Susanny" on those rare occasions we 'uns had leisure time for such."

"Well I believe I could try to hum along if you've a mind to keep whistling and me able to draw breath enough."

All around were views and visions of such a spectacle of

nature. Looking back downslope we could still make out some groves of aspen with early spring leaves shimmering in the soft breezes. The atmosphere captivated us in an interlude of pure clarity.

But alas, the solitude was abruptly disturbed by a fellow coming down towards us from the ridge line. His sudden appearance gave me quite a start.

"Howdy, pilgrims!"

"And hail to you!" Otis called back.

"Name's Father Dyer. If you have any letters or such I can stash them into my satchel."

"I have a letter someplace in my pack needing to be sent to my people back in the Old Country. I've had no news of them since before crossing the Mississippi, seems like a lifetime ago. My animal will give me permission to search for it inside this pannier. If I ask him real nice and sweet. Let me just get it out." I said.

"I'm Otis Walls and this be my partner Jasper Gratz. We're headed to the gold fields over in California Gulch. What's your story, and why called 'Father', do you say?"

The man was dressed in a suit of dark clothes, unlike miner's garb. His age hard to read, but tufts of grey hair stuck out from under a wide brimmed black hat. His countenance was resolute and serene.

"I'm a mail carrier and a preacher to all in these scattered mining camps. I hail from Fairplay down bottom of this here pass and I sometimes lodge around Buckskin Joe. In wintertime I snowshoe with long boards strapped to my feet. Don't matter much to me when storms are raging. I know the way with my eyes shut tight."

Reaching into his pouch he pulled forth a well-worn Bible. "Be my pleasure to read out a passage or two from The Good Book."

The preacher didn't wait for any reply from us before he set to reading from the New Testament.

Otis and I exchanged a look and plopped ourselves down on a sizable boulder. Didn't seem to us a passage would hurt our sensibilities.

I threw a look in Pepper's direction hoping that a somber message might would seep into his thick skull.

The readings ended but the preacher continued to hold our attention. "You men ever heard tell how this here trek come to be known as Mosquito Pass?"

We both shook our heads "no".

"Well there's a story says some gents from parts around California Gulch got together to straighten out some mining disputes as well as to name this here pass. They couldn't decide, so set up another meeting to be held a week hence to settle the question. One of the men had a ledger for figuring numbers and keeping records of one sort or another. And so opens it to the page where there was a blank space to be filled in. And right there on that blank line was a squished mosquito. And that name stuck for all time."

Otis and I exchanged a second look sure that this was something of a tall tale. But we kept quiet.

Time had been passing quickly as we spent hours with the preacher. In fact we had a late afternoon sun beginning to tip over the ridge. Checking my shirt pocket I realized that I had but half a plug of chew left to my name.

"We've had ourselves quite a day. Might just set up a camp near that outcrop up yonder. Looks to be at the edge of a span of plateau, grassy and a stream flowing through. How much time to the summit, do you think, Preacher?" All this from Otis.

"Oh. Hour and a half, two, maybe." Gazing around at the meadows he added, "Springtime surely brings out all the wildflowers a 'blooming."

The plateau would one day be known as American Flats.

Each one of us took a moment to admire the splendid array of pinks, purples and blues, with lots of yellows mixed in.

So then off we hiked a short distance across a bitty stream and onto the flatter land. 'Course Pepper stopped mid-stream, but I was having none of his nonsense, and gave his rope a firm tug.

Father Dyer turned and watched as we walked a short ways and began to set up a camp.

"Welcome to share our fire if you've a notion." I was enjoying his company quite a lot. And too Otis and I were dragging a stout log to use for sitting on.

"We're running low on meat of late. Fact is we haven't had much to eat for the better part of two days, but you're free to share some taters and Gus here's in possession of a whisky flask."

At this the preacher whipped out a kind of slingshot and dinged a snowshoe hare about a dozen yards away.

"There be something for your supper I'd say, fellows!"

"Well howdy. That's a handy trick if ever I saw one." I said, springing up and fetching the game from a nearby piney bramble.

My companions made fast work of skinning the rabbit while I laid out a fire using some splinters I'd been hauling in my pack for just such a pickle. And as luck would have it I was able to use some pieces of branches broken off a stunted pine which poked out from the hare's lair.

We soon had us a warm fire, game sizzling on a spit and two taters roasting in the embers.

I mused aloud regarding my dwindling tobacco supply and just that quick the preacher produced a pouch and had me help myself. He didn't use the stuff himself he said, but carried it for small trades along his travels.

The latter part of this afternoon had brought a very pleasant turn of events, indeed.

We made a tent once more to use as shelter, but were of a mind to sit around the fire taking nips of the whisky and listening to tales the preacher had no shortage of.

"Well, friends, away back in '62", he began, "there was some doings around South Park. You might have heard tell of the Espinosa gang."

Nope. We hadn't.

"There were some brothers along with their relations from away down in Mexico territory who had a vendetta against the American government claiming it had despoiled their family holdings. These Espinosa fellows were taking out their revenge by terrorizing settlers, robbing them and even killing many. Eventually a posse found the outlaw camp near Fairplay and a gun fight ensued. One of the older brothers was killed but the rest managed to escape. The two younger Espinosa brothers and one cousin vowed revenge once more."

He went on, "A second posse was formed this time using men from both east and west sides of Mosquito Pass and rode after the gang with gusto. The parties encountered one another in a southern section of the Park and one more gun battle erupted. Three of the posse paid with their lives. But every single one of the gang was shot dead, except for one brother who escaped capture and remains at large to this day."

"Well, Preacher Dyer, if I ever cross paths with a man says his name be Espinosa I'll be sure to tip my hat and inquire after his kinfolk." Otis always seems to have a joke up his sleeve.

The weather was frigid that night and left us with a rime of snow on our canvas covering. But the new morning began as fair as could be. The blueness of the sky defied description, but I'll have a go. A deep pure bright blue that if you look hard you could imagine spiraling right into the depths of all that blue.

Pepper and the mule got the last of the hardtack. My burro looked to be satisfied but I couldn't trust him worth a plug nickel. I didn't like the shiftiness of his gaze no-how. And sometimes I swear I could detect a smirk on his lips.

"Um, say, Preacher. Do you have a practical prayer to deliver over a domesticated animal? My burro seems to be full of the devil, so to speak. I'd sure be obliged if you could give 'er a try."

"Methodist is what I was schooled to be. Sure ain't no papist but I have heard tell of a saint called Francis who's a friend of all creatures. I'll ask him for a favor. Don't know if he works for the opposition, though."

And with this the good Father Dyer spoke some words into Pepper's ear. Have to wait and see on that one. I've not known orneriness in man nor beast like that of my burro.

Before we said our good-byes to one another and readied to set out in our separate directions, Otis mentioned the busted crates of vegetables.

"If you've a way to carry them you should stop and pick up those taters, turnips and rutabagas to take along to Alma. Some miner's wife might cook up a tasty stew and gladly share it with you."

"Uh huh. Might. Though I'm just now thinking to go by way of Buckskin. Someone may have what's known as an express delivery to be taken on down to Fairplay."

"What might that be, express delivery?" I asked.

"A miner will pay handsomely to have a pouch of gold dust carried to a local-type bank or vault and from there put on a stagecoach to Denver City. It's an easy way to add to my wages."

"Yes, well just keep a sharp eye out for banditos!" Said Otis.

"Have a prosperous year men. I maybe will see you on one of my future rounds."

Many months went by before we saw Father Dyer again.

The preacher's estimate of two hours to reach the summit was on the more generous side. Because not twenty minutes from this last campsite we were faced with a colossal snow field, one that could not be skirted around. I stepped out onto it and found it solid enough to hold my weight. Tugging on Pepper's rope I pulled him along. But he sank right in and stood there looking at me.

"Oh no. Don't even think about having things your own way. Just follow me, you hear?"

All in our outfit angled along in a diagonal line sometimes sinking a foot or so down but not with every step. This was difficult work but we didn't allow for any discouragement. The day continued fair and sunny, so no significant complaints. More and more the higher we climbed we had dirt and rocks under foot as the wind had blown the snow off in a consistent manner. As we were tackling a slope of talus we saw five or six small sized birds strutting nearby with feathers half white and the others brown. One had a brood of chicks in her wake.

Otis said, "Ptarmigans. Feathers are all white in winter. You might have seen their cousins out on the plains called grouse, but better known as good eating."

"Yes sir. I do recall the youngsters in our train using slingshots to hunt grouse and sometimes turkeys. More than a time or two the women folk had one a roasting on a spit."

Presently we singled one out, wrung its neck and tied it to Otis' mule.

At last we reached the summit of the pass and sat down using a rock outcrop as a windbreak. This gave us a vantage point for studying the hills and gulches on the pass's west side. First thing I noticed were some high mountains against the western horizon. They were splendid, magnificent, glistening with snow. Next thing caught my attention were all the good trees covering the hillsides below. With just some patchy snow banks remaining.

We both noticed a single cabin several hundred yards away. Looked to be substantial and solid. Smoke coming out a stone chimney and logs stacked up on the sides.

We moved on down the hillside and approached the sturdy cabin making lots of racket so as not to startle the occupant and cause him to load up a shotgun.

"Hail the cabin!" Hollered Otis.

Presently a fellow emerged looking rather queer in red longjohns, hat on head and Sharps in hand.

"Howdy. Wonder if we might sit a spell and inquire about a thing or two." Said Otis.

It suited me to have my friend take the lead in these encounters, as he had a direct way of chatting up strangers.

The man was slow to answer. Took considerable time studying us, looking over the animals, and checking out our ptarmigan. After a while he ambled back into his cabin and returned dressed in overalls, flannel shirt and tall boots. Hat still on his head topped a considerable length of dark hair and side whiskers. He leaned his rifle against an outside wall, which put me more at ease.

"Name's Jake Morgan. What be yours?"

"Otis Walls and this greenhorn is my partner Jasper Gratz. We're wondering if a trail marks the way into California Gulch. I've been there once or twice before but those times my approach was by way of Weston Pass and Granite."

"Well, just keep a going downslope southerly. Bring you to Upper Oro where they's lots of been building happening. Last I heard a boarding house with baths provided and another saloon. Tabor's got a store with a fine array of goods. Even some cans of fruit sometimes.

"Haven't been there myself since last fall. Had us some heavy snows here about that kept me from striking out for weeks on end. Matter a fact one storm didn't let up for the better part of ten days."

Our pack animals had been pawing at some sooty snow so as to get at the grasses underneath.

"Set yourselves down on this here log bench. I'm boiling up some coffee and free to partake. And look it here, these skillet biscuits are just now cooked and ready to eat. Jasper, boy, you got something there on your face needs wiping off."

I said what I always have. "Born with the mark."

We both thought the meal was a very fine offer and went to our pokes for our tin cups and then held them out to be filled. Had us two biscuits apiece. The sun was almost directly overhead reminding us not to tarry overlong as we yet had a long hike ahead of us.

We visited with Jake, a Brit, for a while longer. He was speaking of two miners whose cabin we would be passing along the way.

"Can't say as I know them very well. Said they're from Ireland. One can sing the pigs out of the hills, so to speak. They have some workings down slope over in Iowa Gulch the other side of what's called Breece Hill, the Long and Derry, and once the snow melts completely noise from their blasting will fill the air even clear over to here and about."

"Jake, your mention of Tabor brought to mind a story I read in a letter back in my home country some years ago. A good woman living in the settlement of Auraria, name of Augusta Tabor, ministered to my kinsman who'd been suffering from a malady of the lungs. Could this be the same Tabor do you know?"

"Yes, it is the same person, I reckon. She's a hard working

woman. Everybody says so. Mrs. Tabor been seeing after the needs of many who ventured into the gold fields. She runs a store and post office while her husband gallivants around politicking and prospecting. She's handy with the sewing needle they say and the wash tub. Top it all off she has a youngster to keep track of."

"Good to know." I stood and knocked my hat against my leg. Dusty.

And then, "Before we take our leave would you describe the way of building a cabin such as yours? Could two such as we be complete a modest dwelling in say a month?" I wondered aloud.

I'd been musing off and on about how Otis had been a'telling folks that he and I be partners. Well, I'll be going right along with his idea. I could use all the help available for this new life ahead.

"Sure is time of year for such a venture. I finished this here cabin about twelve months ago, pretty near exactly this very month. I have marked off on an inside wall every day and month that I have lived on this hillside. I use sun rises for keeping track. Not scientific but a record of sorts."

Jake continued, "And I'll just say by way of explaining how a cabin goes up that there's all manner of temporary dwellings a person could construct. One is a bough house which you'd pile stacks of branches one over another to keep the coldest of winds out. Or some will burrow into a hillside and stack logs on the front side only. To either of these structures a stone fireplace can be built within. Of course comfort is a whole other matter what with adding beds and cupboards and such. As far as practicality goes either would only do for one winter season at most. "

Otis and I sat and thought all this out. There was much to consider and we hadn't been partnered up for all that much time, so our thinking might likely go in opposite directions.

When Otis eventually spoke up I found myself agreeing.

"Might be Jasper and me will make use of the boarding house over in Oro City for a few weeks or so and then be more disposed to choose a path forward."

"Thanks to you, Jake, for such a warmth of welcome and hospitality." I said.

"I do like visits and friendly company. And if you decide to cabin-build you'd be welcome to use my whipsaw for slab logs and any other tools I might could loan out. Of course my expert advice would be freely given. "

After checking our gear and animal packs and in Otis' case, an unwieldy sledge type outfit, we set off once more. The afternoon remained fair and our route took us almost to the vicinity just above the Long and Derry cabin. We didn't encounter the Irishmen and so kept up a steady pace.

The terrain was much like the east side of Mosquito Pass, but before long we had dropped well below tree line and the scents of the forest along with the softness of pine needles underfoot suited us favorably. Turning to look at Pepper I saw in him a most agreeable demeanor. Good.

Arrival in California Gulch.

Early evening found us dropping down into California Gulch. We stopped beside a good sized tent where some fellows in a swept yard were barbering one another.

Before all else, I had the notion to tie Pepper to a tree. But as I approached the fiend from behind, he surprised me with a kick from his rear legs. He about got me in the head but I ducked and the blow glanced off my shoulder. An unfounded trust of my burro would be a caution to me in the future. For now I swallowed back tears of pain mixed with fury.

Not a person, including Otis, had witnessed Pepper's show and my humiliation. Whew! I scooped a fistful of snow from a lingering sooty mound and rubbed at my soreness vigorously.

Otis having noticed a stove spewing smoke right there in the clearing approached the men. "Howdy! My partner here and myself have a handsome bird needs roasting. We'd be happy for all to partake if we might could use that cook-stove over yonder for the task."

Of the half dozen men standing about the yard two or three heads turned our way and showed only slight interest. The others went about the business of loitering around the area. Far as I could tell from the many half cut logs scattered about on all sides of the tent it appeared there were plenty of chores could be taken care of by idle hands.

The one holding a razor to the cheek of another finished his ministration and then slowly wiped the soap from his instrument onto a soiled towel tied around his waist.

The cleanly shaven man moved off the stump and quick as that another took his place. The barber started in on this next man's shaggy beard.

"Just neat it up, Willy, and maybe trim the hair back of my neck."

Not a single one of them had bothered to address us yet, so I gave in and offered a fare-thee-well. "Well, then, we'll take a turn on down into the gulch and not trouble you men further."

Otis and me ambled back toward our animals and gear but were brought up short by a fellow squatting next to the stove and sporting a tattered vest with a badly used bowler on his head.

He said, "Tell out your names and intended purpose. As for the friendly loaning out of our appliances we first aim to gather some facts. Just be aware we won't be sharing with scoundrels."

"We be Jasper Gratz and Otis Walls from the other side of the Pass. Anyone who has come that way knows what difficulties must be overcome before calling the trip a success. And just now we have a mind to take our chances with finding some color."

The man's name was Charlie Turner and he granted us some unsolicited information. His voice was gravelly and his face scowling. He was generally brooding and repulsive.

"The gold's been played out in this here gulch for some time. Matter of fact, Clyde and George here were happy enough finding some specks in their sluice. But how long ago was it?"

"Back almost two years, I reckon." Said George, spitting a brown stream of tobacco juice into the woods.

Clyde grunted his agreement. His teeth were as yellow brown as George's; each had a puffed out cheek from the telltale habit of chewing.

The revolting Charlie Turner said, "Most men have been working shifts in the Printer Boy for $2.50 a day. Us too some days. But the work's too hard and the pay's too stingy. "

We had heard hints of this before, but it was clearly unwelcome news as we had been counting on finding some nuggets in a pan. And so the two of us solemnly sat ourselves down on logs ruminating.

"Here now, then, the matter of our use of your stove. What's it to be?" Otis asked. I was remembering the good biscuits we'd eaten several hours before; he was likely thinking this too.

The miner who now sported a clean shaven face was the one called George Kilpatrick. He offered this bit of instruction. "It would take a full day to roast such a large fowl in that stove, don't draw worth a damn." He spit a stream of tobacco juice into the dirt and some of it dripped down over his chin. He swiped it off with his hand before continuing.

"Now if it were me had that there bird I'd say pull the feathers and stuff the cavity with clean snow, then take it over to Doc Brut's eating house and have the cook roast it. Tell him it's a token gift of sorts. That way you'll eat good today and maybe one more meal for free the morrow."

I lifted my eyebrows and looked for a reaction from Otis who nodded his assent, and then I said, "What say you all join us for such a repast? Being as you've been a welcoming party for us, we'd like to show our 'preciation."

Willy, the barber, now spoke up, "Fact be we have the rump portion of a deer yet frozen in our ice cave up yonder, so we'll be eating a slice of venison steak this night. Some of us might be seeing you again if you've a mind to stick around the Gulch for a time."

This comment seemed to us a dismissal and so we said "Hidey ho!" We then went back to our pack animals, me pointedly coming at Pepper from his front, untied them and took the winding southernmost trail out of the camp.

We walked over a small rise and from this vantage point could see several wooden structures perched on both sides of a rough wagon road. Numerous log cabins. Directly below us was a small water wheel turning a saw. Walking a ways further along the road a substantial looking lodge built with logs might could be the earlier mentioned boarding house. A small lean-to with railings struck us as a handy place to tie our animals.

Once inside the atmosphere was close and heavy with human smells. The light was smudgy from a lack of windows, but a man of stature approached us. He was dressed in trousers paired with braces and vest. His dark hair neatly combed and mustache nicely trimmed.

"I'm Doc Brut and welcome to my establishment, a place for eating and sleeping. I'm just now overseeing the sweeping out of detritus from a week of boarders who filled every inch of space. They'll be clamoring to get back in here before too long."

"We be Otis Walls and Jasper Gratz. Hoping to set up quarters before looking for work in the lode mine or maybe the stamp mill."

"You'll have to wait until Buster whacks the bell before you can be offered accommodations. Just as the sun is setting. Most men line up early to be sure of a space."

"Thanks for the good suggestions, Mr. Brut." I said.

"It's Doc. Just Doc."

"Say, we have this here handsome fowl to hand over for roasting, free of charge. Or maybe to pay for our board for one night." Said Otis.

"The bird's a fine idea. I'll send Buster out front to see about it. You fellows be sure to get an early place in line, and then we'll see about beds for the night."

"Thanks to you, Doc."

Buster approached directly to inspect the bird. He grunted his approval, so we handed it over to him.

Back out on the street we looked about. All was noise and hustle especially coming from the saloon next door. The two of us had a notion to go in for a whisky but we lacked the cash for such. So instead we procured a bucket so as to carry water for our animals.

A friendly guy near the stream handed us some feed he had in a flour sack. Said he'd lost his mule and wouldn't be needing it; then he told us he was flush from a night of gambling and felt like sharing his luck.

"Hold up for a dang minute, will you?" I said.

"Ja?"

"You sound like folks from my village Aachen in Germany. Does that ring a bell?"

"I'd say so. You bet. My uncle lives in that place. My name's Bakke, Samuel Bakke."

"Well, I'll be! Ain't that just something! How long you been in this here gulch?"

"Been round here since 66, I guess. Spent a deal of time around Cache Creek down where they found gold near Granite. My brother, Fritz, got killed in a stagecoach holdup three years ago."

"That be some bad news to have to send home. I'm Jasper's partner, Otis Walls."

"We have to take care of our pack animals, but come into Doc Brut's and eat some supper with us, Samuel. We have much news to share I'd say. My family name is Gratz, by the way."

"That's a swell idea. I'll join you at sunset if that suits." Then he just stood there staring at us, maybe tracking the name Gratz in his memory.

"You go on now. We'll be along by and by." I said, and we headed back to the animal lean-to.

"What do you think of that, huh, Otis? Meeting someone from

my very own village and so far from Germany. It leaves my head reeling with the wonder of it."

"Strange happenings is all I can think. And that be the god's truth."

Otis' mule and Pepper were standing tied to the rail right where we'd left them. I was careful to circle around to the front and then offer the pail first to the mule and second to my burro.

"You don't need to think I would give you a gift out of the blue, fool animal. I'm still smarting from the kick you gave me. But this windfall came from a man doesn't even know you. So eat up 'fore he comes along and sees what a shameless creature you truly be, and wants it back."

Otis was busy deciding what to do with the items from the wrecked wagon. He knew he must figure out how to pay back the freight outfit for the lost goods. Something that hadn't even crossed my mind.

"What say we take these tools to that mercantile store before we go to Doc's for supper, Jasper? Maybe change them for cash money so we can at least buy us a whisky tonight."

"We'd better get a 'going then or run late at the boarding house. Pile those three shovels and the double jack on my arms. You can get the rest, can you?"

"Yep."

Just up from Doc's place we stepped into a good sized log building. A store with all manner of shelves built onto the walls. Crates and barrels were anywhere and everywhere. There were so many smells I couldn't separate them in my head; some were pleasing while others made my eyes smart.

Besides all manner of food stuffs: rice, wheat flour, dried beans, lard in buckets, molasses, and coffee, we could see every kind of tool and implement; most items were difficult to make out in the dimness of the room. We approached a long wooden counter top where a neatly dressed woman was helping a customer. Before long the man left with his goods.

"Afternoon, Ma'am. Hoping to trade these items if you have need for such in your store. We've hauled them all this way from down by Alma, but it's hard to keep our eyes on them in such a busy town. Reckon they'll get took before we can find a way to safeguard them." Said Otis.

"Put them down over in this corner, and I'll inventory the lot. Three shovels, two picks and two double jack hammers. I guess I can give you a ten dollar bag of gold dust. That's all we use for currency around these parts. Sure you don't want to hold on to some tools for work in the placers?"

"No. Right now we need cash money so as to get ourselves settled in. More than likely we'll be back here once we get us some work."

"Well then I'll go ahead and weigh the dust. Matter of fact, this is the only gold weighing scale in the Gulch. You can watch if you like; you'll see we give a square deal in this store." The woman said.

"Thank you most kindly, Ma'am." We took the gold dust

and left.

"Here. Put the bag under your hat for now, Jasper. We'll find a more secure hidey-hole after supper. Got to remember to hold back some dust to pay the freighters."

And then we walked over to the front of the boarding house where the smoky scent of roasting fowl was in the air. A dozen men were already lining up. We studied them from under the brims of our hats; all were in miners' garb in various states of disrepair; shabby and filthy.

Samuel Bakke was near the front nattering away with Doc when he spotted us and moved back to where we were standing in line. Didn't have time to say more than howdy when a clanging bell set the place churning with men as they swarmed and nudged to get a spot in line.

"Watch your brash manner, fellows. Any shenanigans and you'll get booted to the back of the queue." Said Doc, loudly.

We shuffled inside and Doc led the troops to a back section where the dirt floor was covered with hay and straw. Men were quick to stake out a spot before ambling off to the benches and eating tables.

Oh, but us three were led into a little enclave and told to leave our coats and small bundles on top of some piney boughs. Doc mentioned that lookouts walked around making sure no one be victimized in his establishment. This information set our minds at ease, not that we owned anything of worth 'cept the gold pouch still hidden under my hat.

Then Doc bade us find a place on the benches at the front part of the building. As soon as we were settled I took to quizzing Sam about his brother for starters.

"A stage holdup three years ago, you say?" I began.

"Me and Fritz were real low on funds, hadn't had much luck finding any gold here or anywhere, even Cache Creek. So we heard about express delivery as a way to earn some cash, and we decided to sign up for the work."

"Hey, Jasper and me met up with a preacher name of Dyer who did this kind of job now and again." Said Otis.

"Yes. I've seen the parson a few times. Went to one of his preaching meetings once over in Tabor's store."

Sam was slow getting started telling about his brother's murder; maybe it was difficult for him to look back and think about it. Also, his German accent was hard for Otis to follow and this slowed him down.

"Well, we had to tramp clear over to Buckskin to get the gold dust and then hopped on the stagecoach heading for Fairplay. On arriving there the gold was placed in a secure location before being sent on to Denver City. First time everything went along without a hitch. Our take was $20 and we were most satisfied with the whole setup."

The story telling stopped while large bowls of steaming beans and pans of cornbread were placed on the tables. Each man had been supplied a tin plate and spoon that he could use as his own for as long as room and board was paid for. The next part of the meal created quite a hubbub when the servers brought out pots of gravy with particles of roasted fowl floating on top. It was quite a feast, almost as if a holiday had been declared. The room was very gay.

"So what happened, Samuel?" I asked.

"It was only the second time for us on that job and the stage had five passengers besides me and my brother. The trunk strapped to the top was meant to be a decoy while the real payroll was tied under the driver's seat. Fritz and I had side arms but neither of us was much of a shot. The only sharp shooter was riding shotgun holding his rifle next to the driver.

"We were only two miles from Alma when the ambush happened. Four riders came galloping from the forest and the head man took hold of the lead horses to stop us. The coach was left vulnerable when two of the bandits put bullets into the driver and the rifleman, who hadn't even shot off a round. So sudden and well planned was the assault that none of the men sitting inside had a chance to draw his weapon. Except Fritz. He was able to wing one of the outlaws but got shot through his heart for his trouble.

"Then after dislodging the trunk and finding nothing within, the robbers soon discovered the hidden gold sacks, tied them to their saddle horns, and rode back into the trees without a backward glance at those of us lying there, hogtied on the ground."

We sat there speechless having long since finished with supper.

After a time Otis suggested that Sam go get his belongings

and sleep the night with us. He was mighty agreeable to this plan.

I went over to Pepper's stall to see that all was well for the night. I gave him a pat on his nose which was countered with a sullen bray. He has such a churlish attitude.

I retrieved Otis' poke along with my own and met up with him in a very raucous saloon. He was now on his second whiskey so then we drank one down together. I handed over a pinch of dust to the barkeep and we took our leave.

Once more back at Doc's we saw my countryman loitering with Buster the cook and sauntered over that way.

"Why not settle in for the night and when it comes daybreak we can become further acquainted?" I said.

All agreed and when we found our sleeping space tucked in the back of the building, fell asleep instantly.

I awoke to the smell of hay and greasy fried meat. Arising with a bit of stiffness I carefully stepped over Sam and Otis but within minutes the two joined me at an eating table. Platters of gamey meat and biscuits and blackened pots of coffee to wash it down were to be the usual fare. We greeted a friendly Doc as he made rounds about the room and then took our leave.

Once more out on the dusty road Otis and I attempted to draw Sam into a conversation but he seemed reluctant to do so. After agreeing to meet up later in the day for a whiskey, he took his leave.

And then the two of us started off.

"What say we set to exploring this here gulch after we see to the animals?"

"Okay by me. I'm more than curious what we'll find further down. We keep hearing of placer claims being reworked. I'd like to see for myself." Said Otis.

Filling the bucket with water at the creek and trying to walk without sloshing it was tricky. As Pepper was dipping his nose into the bucket his ears pricked up and I became alert immediately. A stranger approached with stealth and Otis who'd been behind the mule and hidden from view spoke and startled the fellow.

"What can we do you for, Pilgrim?"

"Just getting my bearings. Come to see what's what in the Gulch this day."

He had a shiftiness to him. His overalls were covered with more holes than cloth and his black hat was in tatters, the wide brim torn half off. After studying our situation he seemed to come to a decision but then turned and sauntered away. We both recollected seeing this fellow at the busy tent site a few days back.

"Better keep a lookout for that fellow. He seems to be a no account and acts kind of barmy."

I nodded my agreement. After untying our animals we set off to survey the surrounds.

A Place to Work

We hiked along the road where we'd been the day before and counted four saloons, a second store, and two more boarding houses. Also a poorly constructed brothel, which in truth was a lean-to covered by some tenting, and three cribs for lacquered girls . Noisy laughter poured onto the road from a gambling hall and someone was playing an out-of-tune piano in a seedy looking saloon the next door down. All this noise seemed to assault the senses so early on a sunny morning.

Now it seemed to us that one mile ran into another and another after that. Chipmunks chattered and a large jay squawked from a bitty stand of aspen. Nothing new to study on the hillslope side but there were some dozen placer miners working at their sluice boxes down by the streams.

We kept a 'going another mile down the deeply rutted road and found ourselves at the bottom of the gulch where the hills appeared to flatten out. Our eyes were drawn to the bright white of the mountains across a wide valley floor. Spring thawing had begun on the high peaks but just by looking at them we could tell there was a plentiful amount yet to melt into the Arkansas. The dazzle made us squint our eyes into slits.

We then noticed a rather large log house a ways to the southwest and we headed on over to it.

A fellow with a friendly demeanor was carrying some sizable

boards in his arms and stopped some distance from us before dropping the load. Two large, shaggy dogs set to barking but were penned up on the side of the house.

Otis called out, "Howdy, friend!"

I am always taken by surprise at Otis' agreeable approach to strangers.

However, at the moment I had my hands busy tugging Pepper along. He was acting unreasonable again. I had no notion of what was setting him off at the moment. Could be the clamor of the hounds. Could be his own inner voice nudging him to try some rascally trick.

"Don't you even dare - I'm warning you!" He nudged my backside but didn't push hard. I figured this was one of his ways of showing off.

"Tom Starr." He said. A stocky man with dark brown hair about medium height. He was outgoing in manner and held out his hand to shake with us.

"Some of these here sluices belong to you?" Asked Otis.

"Yep. And others over in Iowa Gulch. I hire on some men when I need help. Have not need of too many these days. The gold's about near gone. I spend time blacksmithing, too; although I'm not very good at it." Starr added.

"So what jobs are men doing to feed and shelter themselves?"

"Some's hired on to mine a lode up yonder way, name of Printer Boy. Hard rock takes a lot more muscle and sweat than placer, I know; but talk is the mine owners need considerable help getting the gold from out the quartz. But myself, I'm just now in the business of rewashing the placers. Scoop up some of the specks left behind in haste by earlier prospectors."

"Well, much obliged for all the information. We're set on getting jobs in that Printer Boy mine one day soon, least I am. Sam and Otis here would likely be able to lend a hand at the rewashing you mention." I said.

"Welcome to come around this coming up Sunday. Reverend Robinson is set to say Mass for all that wants to attend. Right here in my house."

"We might just will show for such doings. Speaking for us all it's been a mite too long since we've attended a church-like service." Said Otis.

The dogs set to howling after us as we started on back up the road. Mr. Starr shouted out to hush them.

The road we walked was sometimes mud but mostly yellowish dust and rocks. At least during these summer months. Anytime a freight wagon passed we turned our heads away coughing as the wheels whipped up clouds of dust. If a rider was galloping on his horse to get up or down the Gulch in a hurry clouds of road dust got stirred up. Just now I cocked my head to study the northern hillside where a doe and her fawn were nibbling grasses.

Otis was of a mind to take his Sharps out, but I told him we didn't need the work of dressing out game this late in the day. Pepper took no heed of the forest animals but he did take a notion to change his slow walking gate to a canter and I was forced to run like the devil to keep up.

"Stop, I say!" And when Otis came even with me he helped to jerk on my burro's rope. The two of us managed to put a halt to this latest behavior.

"What the heck was that all about?" I wondered aloud.

"Might be he thinks his dinner is waiting."

"Might. He sure thinks the world belongs all to himself and his whims, Otis. What say we water and feed the beasts and then get us some supper at Doc's?"

When we went back over to Doc's we had to join a line of roughly clad miners coming in for the evening from various sluices. We saw Samuel up ahead and called to him to move to the back with us.

"What's doing, friend? You been working somewhere about?"

"Hey, Otis, Jasper. Can't say I've been working. Just sweeping up in Tabor's store and dusting the shelved goods. Earned me a pinch of dust, though. The Mrs. T. is always fair in her ways."

Just as Buster whacked his bell we settled at the table, all three swallowing down juices in anticipation of the meal. I had to leave the place to spit out my chew into the street and before long the steaming bowls were placed on the table. This evening it were beans and biscuits and nothing extra.

"See, Jasper, we sure could've brought in that deer from earlier and had meat with this supper."

"Next time, Otis, I won't argue. But it should be a buck, not a doe and youngster. What say we climb back over to Jake Morgan's cabin one of these days?"

"I'd come along. Where is this cabin?" Asked Samuel.

"Just this side of Mosquito Pass down from where it tops off. We didn't walk but thirty minutes from those boulders, did we, Jasper?"

"That's my recollection. Morgan seems a real helpful sort; said he'd assist us with building ourselves a cabin. Supply tools as we'd need them and such." And I silently thought that I'd sure like nothing better than to build a snug cabin and call the place home.

"My thinking is we ought to line us up with some work before we do much else. We're about played out, except the few pinches of dust left from selling the tools at Tabor's. What say you to that?" I added.

"Could be the Printer Boy's hiring. But hard rock mining is mighty rough work." Said Sam.

"Well we're none of us strangers to sore muscles and blisters, I'd say. With my knowhow as a smithy, though, I might get on at the Printer Boy sharpening drill bits and such. Tom Starr replanted this seed in my head."

After supper I went over to the animals to see them settled for the night. "You're a heap more trouble than you're worth, Pepper, and you know it too, don't you? But I'm growing used to having you with me, I guess. I'd sure like to get you schooled in how to behave nice, though."

The burro's reply, a snuffle and jerk of his head.

Later the three of us met up at the saloon for a whisky. Sam was buying. Afterwards we headed to Doc's and our beds. The odors were fierce with so many unwashed bodies mixed in with leftover cooking smells. But as usual we were too tired to pay much mind.

Next morning I shook myself awake and noticed that my friends were already up and gone. I hustled along to get some breakfast, coffee at least.

"Morning, Doc. Mean to give you some money for bed and food. Shouldn't be more than two days hence fore that happens if it suits you."

"Oh, I reckon you boys aren't the sort to run off without paying up. I can give you a few days, sure."

"Say. You happen to see Otis and Sam a while ago?"

"They was going for baths around the bend at the fancy house. It's more than sporting with the offering of a bath for those who have some dust."

"Thanks. Appreciate the update. Think I'll go along and see about a bath for myself. It has been a many long months since my last one, down in Auraria when I first set eyes on the jagged peaks."

"See you gents by and by then.'

"Yep. That be right, Doc." And I moved on to the corral for a quick check on Pepper. All I got for my attention to him was a flinty look in his eyes.

Song birds were playing chase with each other up around the aspen groves and I swatted a buzzing bee away from my face. This was a mighty fine morning with an abundance of sunshine and blue, blue skies. I tipped my hat further down over my eyes so as to shade them.

I walked along with a small bundle of clean and unworn clothes and felt satisfied and hopeful about life here in California Gulch. As I neared the place with a sign "Baths 1 dollar" I saw Otis sitting on a log in front of an all-purpose business (gambling, drinking and sporting girls) holding his face up to the sun's rays, his hair dripping. His visage looking swarthy as usual.

"Hey, ya! Didn't know the plan about baths today, but think I'll head on in for one myself. It's been awhile since arriving in these mountains that I've been clean head to toe."

"Um huh. Feels like rejuvenation, fancy word for fresh and good smelling, Jasper."

"Right, and see you after. Here's Sam all fresh except for his clothes. Need a pinch to get you some new clean pants and shirt, Sam?"

"Yeah. We'll use the last of our dust to get you gussied up." Said Otis.

"Nah. These'll do for a good while yet. I'm going to look into Tabor's store. See if the Missus will scrub them up for me. See you over to the corral in a while."

The sun had moved along in the deep blueness 'fore we three met up again. We agreed that we'd wait an additional day before hunting up jobs and instead hike on up to Morgan's cabin. See what's what.

Along the way after scrambling to the top of a steep embankment I figured to have a talking to with ol' Pepper, who wasn't even bearing a pack saddle this trip but kept pulling backwards on the rope.

"See here, burro! You go when I say go!! I'm of a mind to haul you back to the corral and enjoy my day without your orneriness."

Just to verify his self-importance Pepper actually curled his lip, a smile of sorts, and nuzzled my hand. It is definitely a love-hate connection I feel for this creature.

We skirted up and through some fragrant pines and came into the clearing where several days ago some fellows had been barbering one another.

"Hi ho, the camp!" Said Otis.

Couple men were standing around the cook stove in the cluttered yard, each one holding a cup of coffee. None had a friendly attitude, but Otis and me remembered the same surliness from the first encounter. Otis was never put off by such, most times. 'Course Samuel stood back a ways looking flummoxed.

But then what do you know! Around from behind the tent came that tattered man who menaced us at the Oro City corral.

"Thought we'd seen you somewheres before," I said. "Can't quite recall your name."

"You're too tender with that burro. He needs a good quirting now and again. Name's Charlie Turner. You all get along now. We don't have time for sitting around jawing."

He didn't hold back speaking up for the others in the yard.

"Sorry to bother. So long."

Otis was always civil and as such had enemies few and far between.

The hike back towards Jake Morgan's cabin was strenuous. This direction took us mostly uphill. We had to skirt around a good sized gulch to save some time. Sagebrush grew abundantly all over these stony hills. We were too spent for much talking. I took note of a tiny rodent that Otis said was a pika. It sat chattering on a rock. The sound emitted from this small creature lingered on the breeze for some minutes.

After an hour or so of scrambling up one side of a wildflower strewn incline and down another I asked my friends could we stop and take a breather. Agreement.

"I seem to recall that stand of pines up yonder on that hill and the stream spilling down. Isn't that near to Jake's place?" Otis asked me.

"Seems so. What say you about that Charlie Turner fellow?"

Sam spoke up. "I wouldn't want to meet up with he in a dark alley."

"Him not he, Sam. I plan to ask Jake if he knows of such a one. Upstanding or scoundrel." I said, as I spit a stream of tobacco juice into the sage. I'd secretly like to be shake of this habit. But I don't want to state that I will quit and then finding that I can't, have to duck my head with shame.

So on we walked with the glorious blue sky above and nature all around. Smells and colors of late spring filled the landscape. Mountain flowers - lupine, alpine buttercups and columbine carpeted the hillsides. The earth smelled loamy. The sun shone constant and the buzzing of insects filled the air all around.

Another half mile of uphill and evergreens and we could hear the cabin before seeing it. Jake was chopping logs into stove-sized pieces and buckets of mud spackle were scattered here and there in the yard. He was a steady hard worker.

"Howdy do, Jake Morgan! Thought we'd sit awhile and catch up news if you're of a mind to rest an hour from your labors." Otis said.

"Howdy to you. If this don't beat all. I hopped from bed with the first rays this morning and a running through my head was thoughts of how you men might be getting on over in the Gulch." He paused, "and who be this fellow?"

Each of us settled on stumps or logs but before I sat I staked out Pepper near a tree. He was standing in six inches of high meadow grasses and wasted no time cropping and filling his maw.

"This hearty guy is Sam Bakke from my own village in Germany. Ain't that something? We bumped into one another over in Oro and decided to join together in a three-way partnership. Hasn't been enough time to see if it'll work out. Time will be the judge."

"Have you some coffee. It might be burnt after sitting on the fire since early morning, but it'll wet your whistle."

We each poured some, tasted it and tossed it into the sage.

"So you fill in the cracks between logs with the mud, do you?" I was curious about this.

"That's right. If I don't take time to do such I'd be froze inside the cabin walls before the first snow storm showed itself. Just mix me some mud from the stream bottom with animal fat and dried grasses and pack it in. Works real good."

"Say, Jake, we been gnawing on the idea of waiting a month or two before starting work on a cabin for winter. Thought we'd find us some jobs and save back our earnings for supplies. Met a placer miner at the bottom of the Gulch name of Tom Starr who says he's setting up to rewash the sluice boxes from the early days. We could all get this kind of work."

"Well, Otis, your plans are sound enough. Let me just say it would not be prudent to hold off on the cabin for more than five, maybe six weeks at most. That'll put you deep in summer and with times of rain storms and such the days hurry along towards the winter. Don't want to get caught with an unfinished shelter. That's only my opinion though, boys."

"We'll bear that in mind, Jake, but in the meantime..."

Just as I was speaking, Pepper set to snorting, bucking and kicking. I ran and grabbed the halter close to his head but he reared up and tossed me head over heels. I landed with a thud in pine needles, knocked breathless. Braying wildly and stomping my burro darn near pulled free of his stake. When the dust settled and Pepper had calmed we looked about us and saw what had caused all the commotion. A bushy tailed red fox darting away through the aspens down below the cabin.

Once Pepper gets startled by just about any old thing watch out, is my advice.

"Damn nation! I reckon that one has a streak of wild burro in him." This from Jake.

"He does act wild-like at times but I thought it was his personal whims. Maybe he does have a wildness bred in him, Jake. Doesn't excuse his nonsense far as I'm concerned." I said, rubbing the back of my head, and wincing at the pain in my neck and shoulder.

Sam and Otis had been sitting back studying the cabin throughout the fox and burro drama. I went back over and settled in next to them on the log. Picked up the tin cup I'd dropped, but then thought twice about refilling it. Frankly, the coffee didn't taste none too good, kind of like liquid soot. A hummingbird came zipping in close to some reddish Indian paintbrush and a tranquillity settled all around.

"Saw a bruin with a cub up yonder last week. Have to keep an eye out for them and wild cats too in these hills. Mostly they don't care to come too close but it's good to have your Sharps nearby and handy at all times."

Finally Sam spoke up. "What about bandits and scoundrels? Does any of those kinds come around to harry you?"

And Otis remarked, "There's one man loiters around a large tent uphill of the placers. We've seen him couple times. Name's

Charlie Turner, I seem to recollect. There's a shiftiness in his eyes and he sure does have an unfriendly, disagreeable manner."

"Be canny and stay clear of that one. The whole bunch at that tent has been known to ride with the Reynolds gang now and again. Not lately but last year the word was. And Charlie Turner as soon drop you with a bullet if challenged in a hold up. He's one not to turn your back on in most instances. Anyhow I wouldn't trust him at all, not ever."

"Well, glad to know we had the guy pegged as such. But sure bothers me that the others milling around that camp are outlaws. Isn't there a sheriff or lawman anywhere in these parts?"

"California Gulch is a mining district set up legal and a committee of five men operate under what's called Miners' Law. Course their duty is meant to settle placer claim disputes, mostly. Now and then a ruckus in a saloon or gambling hall will be smoothed over by this assemblage." Said Jake.

"So it's live and let live and just try to avoid the lawless men, huh?" I said.

"Most fellows will give you a fair shake and come to your aid if you need defending from a human varmint. That's how I've found things ever since I've been in these hills."

"Tell us, Jake, do you spend days in the Gulch? Maybe just to fill a small pouch so you have dust for a whisky or a game of poker or such?"

"Nope. I did have a placer claim a few years back. But now that the gold is mostly gone from the creeks I have all I need right here in the woods to get by and live satisfied."

And he did behave as if contented. He alluded to a secret cache inside his cabin but made clear that he would not divulge the contents to any living being. He grabbed a broom made from a stout evergreen branch and now used it to sweep around the cabin doorway. Then he turned back to face us sitting there on the log and smiled.

"You fellows need to find some enjoyment in your days. Especially during these warm summertime weeks. Soon enough and before you know it the snows will come blowing and the wind trying its best to freeze you to the very spot you stand on."

The afternoon sun was slipping closer and closer to the western peaks on the horizon and the three of us shook off the leisure feeling we'd had since being in Jake's affable company.

I was first to stand up and stretch my sore back muscles. Jake asked if we were planning another visit with him sometime soon, as he sure did enjoy our stopover today.

We reminded him we had to get us some work and soon, and also repeating that cabin building was on schedule in the foreseeable future. We waved our goodbyes and after collecting Pepper headed back in the direction of the Gulch. We deliberately avoided the trail that we knew to pass near the white tent and instead hiked downwards through stands of aspen with abundant new spring leaves sprouting.

A medium white cloud shaded the sun momentarily and a breeze whipped up a small whirlwind of dry leaves as we made haste to get back over to Doc's and have some supper.

Doc gave us a few more days' credit on room and board. And this helped ease our minds until we could get steady jobs, which would happen in the morrow we assured him.

We rose with the song of birds and breakfasted on coffee, biscuits and beans and then walked into the bright blue-skied morning. So many fine days all in a row.

"I'm going up to the Printer Boy office to see do they have need for a smithy." I said.

"Me and Sam been talking and thinking on it. So now we'll be going back on down to Tom Starr's. See about hiring on for the re-washing of his sluices. See you around sundown."

"Yep." And I stopped at the corral to make sure Pepper was okay for the day. He gave me one of his surly looks but no kicks or brays which was a welcome sign that he would maybe behave polite for a spell.

I stepped into a small lean-to up at the lode mine and spoke to a fellow who called himself the manager, Judson. Didn't act too interested one way or the other whether or not to hire a willing worker, but after studying me up and down had me sign my name to a sheet of paper nailed to a board.

"Follow me and you can talk to the foreman about what work you'll be doing. About an hour from now will show whether you will be coming back tomorrow as a new hire or not."

"Much obliged."

"Maybe. Maybe not."

The foreman turned out to be friendly and welcoming. He had a bald pate under his black stove pipe hat, and a russet beard and mustache. His leathery face showed the damage of days spent out in the high mountain elements. He held out a reddened hand for me to shake.

"Name's Cal Jackson. Happy to show you the ropes. Fact is we've been in need of a blacksmith to keep all the drill bits sharpened. And now the stamp mill has been installed, it'd be your job to grease the fly-wheel and the crankshaft and any other moving parts."

"Jasper Gratz, and glad to make your acquaintance, Mr. Jackson. It is never indifference I feel for tranquil fellows. Seems I've encountered equal numbers of rough and easy folks since arriving in these parts. But I'll not shirk hard steady work, and I'm willing to begin right away if it suits."

Foreman Jackson showed me the ladder to get to the top of the stamp mill where I'd be applying grease. And after I looked over the forge and inspected the tools I'd be using, I was satisfied that the setup would work well.

The remainder of the day found me sharpening drill bits and putting to use a set of heavy steel tongs so as to move the hot steel bits from forge to anvil.

As the sun sank behind the western peaks I removed the leather apron and headed over to see about Pepper. He was acting restless so I tied him to his rope and walked him down to the swiftly flowing stream so's he could dip his snout and drink. I sat on a nearby rock and allowed myself a few minutes of reverie before returning to Pepper's corral and then Doc's.

Otis, Sam and me ate hearty and set off to the saloon down the way for a whisky.

Each of my pards had his own way of telling how the day went, although both had affirmative things to say about Tom Starr and the fair way he managed his sluice claims.

"Way he explained it, most of the abandoned placer claims had been recklessly squandered during the first boom years. So Starr now has a crew rewashing each of these formerly abandoned claims." Said Otis.

"We signed on right there at his cabin, remember, at the bottom of California Gulch? At the end of every day each man pays four bits to Starr from his labors. Pockets any dust he's found. Fair I'd say."

"I'll just say that I think we've all done a mighty good job of finding gainful employment. I do rightly recollect how skillfully Starr had constructed his cabin, Sam. I'd even venture to speculate that we'll have ourselves a sound cabin long before the summer's gone, we three keep a 'working."

We tucked into our straw beds and fell asleep as soon as our heads dropped.

The next few weeks passed with no new challenges. We worked from dawn to dusk and met regular at the end of each day. We were soon able to pay Doc for room and food. And Otis paid the freight company for the lost or ruined goods.

A CABIN

About a month later my unused days off had piled up so that my partners and I could get a start on cabin building. My time off added up to five days. Otis and Sam decided to leave off placer sluicing for a week or more.

Pepper hadn't had a proper walk for some time so I was looking forward to hiking across the hills while leading him on a rope. We had a few supplies including a hammer, nails, and tenting tied to the burro's saddle pack. We started out as the sun was coming over the ridges and once again skirted around the white tent area thus avoiding any unpleasantness from Charlie Turner and that bunch.

Hiking across from Oro City to Jake's cabin generally took somewheres around an hour and a half or maybe two. We got ourselves over there in good stead and the sun was mid-morning warm and soft.

"Hi ya, Jake! It's friends outside your doorstep."

"I'm coming, fellows. Just lacing up my boot strings." And out he ambled, a toon under his breath, and his typical friendly countenance offering each of us a welcome.

"We're all set up to raise a cabin if'n we might borrow your whipsaw." I said.

"Here it is right here. Keep it as long as you need. Can I offer you some coffee and biscuits 'fore you get started?"

"No for now. Fact is I sure would like to have something to show we'd worked hard and steady all day. We'll be around later in the day for some needed refreshment. If that suits." I said.

"Been thinking to put up the cabin just around that knoll over yonder. Handsome stand of aspens and plenty of pines to build with." Said Otis.

A head nod and then, "I'm a 'doing some hunting today. Maybe bag a deer. Then I'll dress her out and smoke and dry most of the meat. Tomorrow or say the day after I'll lend a hand on your cabin if you're still at it."

"You're sure a good man to call friend, Jake." And Sam, Otis and me waved our goodbyes.

We set out around a hillside yonder about 15 minutes from Jake's and scoped out a flat portion then set to work chopping and sawing. Logs were laid out so as to have a building plan to work from. Next, each timber would have a flat side and we put the whipsaw to work for that outcome.

The day's sun was strong and beat down on our heads and backs. Sweat was dripping into my eyes and the rag I used for wiping my face and neck was stuffed deep in a pocket, so my shirtsleeve was put to use instead.

By late afternoon we stopped to assess our labors. We cyphered that twelve stout evergreen trees should be a good start. Once we had some cut down we stacked them all in one place and then headed towards the Gulch, some two miles to the southwest.

"Mighty fine showing for less than a day's work. Tomorrow maybe we gather creek rocks to use for a fireplace. Would take three or four trips but I figure if we'd borrow a mule could cut this portion of the job a mite. What say you to this idea, fellows?"

Some weeks before Otis had up and sold his mule as we'd been strapped for cash at the time. Now we surely were regretting this sale as rash.

Both Sam and Otis were agreeable to renting one and we headed over to the corral, tied up Pepper, gave him some feed and struck out for Doc's.

Some miners were going on about some sporting gals just newly arrived in the Gulch and of a night could be found over at the latest dance hall. One fellow said a new piano box was carried in on the wagon with the gals. There was no fancy house in the Gulch but there were some tented lean-tos the hens used as well as the flimsy whorehouse down the road.

That night while trying to doze off I had thoughts of Lucinda Poole from the westward journey and longed to hear her sweet songbird voice once more. In my mind's eye I conjured visions of her as she looked the evening she sang "Green Grow the Lilacs". Her black hair, hazel-green eyes, and dimpled cheeks. Her terrible sadness when her brand new husband died from snake bite. I now recalled that she had been under the languid indifference of a laudanum drugged mind when I last laid eyes on her.

Morning sun, bright and snappy, greeted us as we left Doc's. First thing we needed to do was find a mule someone might rent to us for the day. I ducked into Augusta Tabor's store to inquire.

Mrs. Tabor was a positive presence in the Gulch and her store offered more than food stuffs and dry goods. She would wash a man's clothes and mend holes in britches for a modest fee. Just this small bit of care made many a miner full of praise for the woman. Sam was one of her happy customers.

"Could ask some of those who loiter near the poker room. They don't seem to have much gumption to work, mule or no." She said.

And fifteen minutes later I hooked up with my mates along with a sturdy mule on a lead rope. The animal was equipped with a pack saddle at the reasonable charge, 25 cents for a long day.

"I told the fellow we'd be needing his mule for a few days at a stretch and he was agreeable to this arrangement, at a higher price of course. What we should do is to take account of how much dust we have between the three of us - before we continue with our enterprise."

"I have two days' wages in my pouch. And I just happen to have a small cache buried under a fallen log up yonder." Said Otis.

"Me. Not so much as all that. Maybe two dollars. Can't seem to hold onto my earnings whenever I pass by a game of 'Three Card Monte'."

'Well, Sam, I believe you're just the sap most scoundrels hope will happen by their table. You know you can't win a crooked game such as that, don't you?" I asked him.

"Well I did see a fellow win a few rounds one night."

"I'll bet he was in cahoots with the dealer. Try not to fall for such scams, okay? Just try is all I'm saying."

And Sam agreed to avoid such temptations in the future, if he could.

"I figure we can pay for a mule for four days. Let's get Pepper and load up some creek rocks before the sun gets too much higher."

As I began to lead Pepper out of the corral he butted my arm away, but I was having none of his contrariness.

"Oh no. Don't give me any of your sass. There's just too much work ahead of us this day. You hear?"

And my burro decided to be cooperative for the time being. But just as I stood there waiting for Otis and Sam an idea struck.

As they approached I asked, "Why not take part of today and hobble together a small wagon, boys?"

"What you got on your mind, Jasper?"

"Well, Otis, I was just now looking over yonder at Mrs. Tabor's store and noticed a couple abandoned wagon wheels. And now the notion's going round and round in my head. A small half wagon would make quick work of hauling creek rocks over to the cabin site."

"I'm all for shortening time spent working on this cabin of ours. I'd like to get back down to the stream rewashing a placer." Said Sam.

"Settled then. Let's meet in front of the Printer Boy office when we've secured the slats and wheels. That way I can use the smithy shop to fasten on the wheels."

And not but two hours later we had a small wagon filled to brimming with rocks and harnessed to our rented mule.

Pepper was hauling additional supplies; but he was never overly burdened for his part of any of our undertakings. We all tended to think of him as a mascot or pet. Suited him just fine and dandy.

Once again at our cabin-in-progress we sorted through what we'd brought along and began work on arranging rocks for a chimney. We used a mix of tarred animal fat, creek sand/clay and dry grasses to use as mortar. And up it went.

"What say we make some tree bough nests to sleep on and not spend precious time traipsing back and forth to the Gulch?" Asked Otis.

Next day was warm like the last several but the sky was filled with thunder clouds. We worked on laying timbers for the side walls and continued layering chimney rocks. We had to take considerable time to dig sandy clay out of a nearby stream bed. Wasn't a whole lot of mud in one spot, so we constantly moved up or down to get enough for a shovel full.

Almost on the noon hour is when torrents of rain bucketed from the clouds. We were soaked in minutes, water dripping from our heads. Nothing about the storm bothered us nor slowed our work, but then a tremendous boom made us jump and duck.

Lightning every few seconds followed by thunder claps.

As if on cue Pepper came galloping by us seemingly being chased by demons; hooves churning up dirt and pine needles and his voice braying louder than could be imagined.

I stood there and watched in complete astonishment. Then I started after him into the trees. My boots couldn't gain purchase on the wet slippery slope and I went sprawling into a hole, not deep but muddy. I felt like letting go with all the cuss words I could think of so as to blast Pepper from here to kingdom come.

The fury of the storm seemed to rage on and on, along with a fury of my own.

When I finally spotted my burro he was downslope hovering in a stand of aspens. He was twitchy and nervous and seemed ready to bolt again at any moment. I approached as calmly as possible and circled round to his front side. However, I felt sympathy rather than fury once I began to speak.

"Okay. I understand your fright at the loudness of the thunder. I'm thinking that this was the reason you spooked and ran. But you'd better get used to rain storms and noisy thunder and lightning because this time of the summer brings a storm each afternoon, I'm told. Now let's get on back to work."

I led Pepper back up a hill of considerable steepness and found Otis and Sam huddled under a corner of tenting which we had plans for at a later time.

"Ho, Jasper, that beast will be the death of you one day. Never seems to have learned much about doing what's expected."

"Well, Otis, I don't know if I agree. His manners have been improving steadily these past weeks and those thunder claps had the three of us all jumpy with nerves. So, I let him off with no scolding this time."

Sam and Otis both grunted their opinions. Not in Pepper's favor.

The storm blew itself to the south and in the stillness that followed we could hear droplets falling from pine branches. Birds were chirping back and forth to each other. The whole of nature had had a cleansing shower and now we were awarded with a display of dazzling splendor. And as a bonus, the air smelled particularly fresh and clean.

We shook rain water from our outer clothes and draped them over sage brush bushes.

"That's one way to wash filth out of our clothes, I reckon." Said Sam.

"It's the hard way. What say we call it a day and go back to Doc's for the night and maybe a hot supper?" I said.

Everyone agreed so we gathered together our damp items and set off.

Once more in the Gulch I took time to tie Pepper to a corral rail. And since I had learned a method of keeping an animal from getting lost I now used a short length of rope with two circles one for each front leg to be stepped into. I used my wiles to trick the burro and before he knew what was going on he was hobbled. I knew that Pepper would not stand for this too often.

He was too savvy. But for now no sudden storm would have him running wild.

Doc was welcoming as always and supper was steaming bowls of beans and hearty slabs of brown bread. We asked Doc to fill us in on the latest news up and down the Gulch.

"Three or four sporting ladies are due to arrive on a stage later this week. Talk is of throwing up a fancy house so's they can be more coddled and content. That tent next to the saloon isn't suitable for these particular sporting gals coming in from St. Louis, not to mention the probability of downright freezing to death once the winter shows itself. Many a man is expectantly awaiting the stage and will gladly lend a hand at raising the whorehouse." He told us.

We agreed that this was eventful but also conceded only moderate interest.

"Far as I know we won't be visiting any fallen angels before our cabin is completely built and ready for winter."

I spoke for my companions as well as myself. Otis and Sam each put on a long face, but I chose not to notice. We had a project that required all of our attention and strong backs and we didn't need no distractions.

One whisky and we settled into our cranny. Truth be told Doc's accommodations weren't a whole lot better than our hastily thrown together beds in the woods. But his friendship and out-going manner was a bonus to be appreciated.

We made the trip across the hills to our cabin several more times during the following weeks. Jake joined us at one point and with his assist progress was apparent. The walls inside and out had to be filled in with the makeshift mortar or the winter would surely creep inside. This reminder was offered by any man we encountered at Doc's.

One day in mid-August we sat outside the cabin putting finishing touches to a table and benches. Otis, Sam and I felt a sense of pride as we sat there.

"Maybe we can stay here permanent-like soon as some bough beds are placed against the walls." I said.

We had some chopped-up logs ready for the large fireplace in the main room. I set a fire going so we could see if it was suitably drawing the smoke up the chimney.

Seemed to each of us that we'd done a proper job of it.

"Mighty fine." Said Otis.

And then Sam parroted this. He'd been repeating what had been said for some time now.

"Look you, Sam. It can be tiresome when thoughts and words get repeated over and over." I told him.

"I'm learning more of the common way folks use the English. If'n I repeat what's being spoke it more likely sticks."

"Um. Well. That's as it should be then."

Otis had been chopping some additional saplings during this exchange. He had a sizable stack there at his feet.

"I'm for building us up some bough beds and then heading on back over to the Gulch before we run short of daylight."

"What did you think we'd do for this night, Otis? Stay here, or go on and come back tomorrow? "

"I'm for going on back, like I said. We need to set up supplies and stock those newly built shelves with goods 'fore we move in permanent like. "

"Ok then that's what we'll do. You agreeable to this plan, Sam?"

He said he was and so after putting together the bough beds we set out once more for Oro City and Doc's.

"Come on you, Pepper. Let's make tracks."

My burro looked up from grazing and shook his head vigorously.

"Well, it's just too bad you feel that way, 'cause we're a going and right now, I say."

Pepper answered with a moderate bray but then decided he'd come along with us. His behavior made me uneasy in my mind, but maybe I shouldn't borrow trouble.

Fifteen minutes later my gut feeling proved dead on. We had just topped the second of the three hills that our trail tracked us over when the burro's rope yanked my arm near out of its socket and my feet flew off the ground. The rope was wrapped too tight around my hand so I was being dragged over sagebrush and I kept trying to brace my feet under me; but Pepper just kept going downslope at breakneck speed.

This was more than spirited vexation – it was a raging madness. Otis and Sam we're chasing after us and just as a large spruce was looming two feet from my face the boys got hands on the rope and ol' Pepper was abruptly yanked to a stop. First thing we noticed was the strong skunk odor. The burro had been sprayed on his legs and was furious about it. I didn't know what to remedy this affront with.

"I say we get the burro over to Oro and maybe see if Mrs. Tabor has any ideas." Said Otis.

"Well let's do it then. The sooner the better. Sometimes I rue the day this animal came into my life."

Doesn't seem we ever made the trip quicker than that afternoon. I tied Pepper to a rail in the corral. No other animals were there at the time, and a good thing too. No doubt the burro would have been most unwelcome.

"Mrs. Tabor. Howdy, Ma'am. Would you have a recipe for ridding a critter of skunk spray?"

"Not a sure-fire treatment, but worth a try, I've been told. Try pouring beer mixed with soap shavings over the sprayed parts. Here's a piece of lye soap. Come back for more advice if need be."

"Mighty grateful, Ma'am. We'll give her a try."

Sam found a bucket and we pooled our dust money so as to buy beer. I got hold of a brush and went to work scrubbing at Pepper's front legs.

After an hour of brushing on the beer and soap mixture Pepper was giving out signals that enough was enough so I left off with the ministrations and stepped outside the corral. I filled my lungs with fresh air and then went back in to test the stink. My burro was not going to win any sweet smelling contests but the stench was not quite as intense as before.

I walked on by the Tabor store and offered a gracious thanks to the generous woman inside. I asked Mrs. Tabor where her husband spends his time, since he never seemed to be about the store premises.

"Mr. Tabor is over at Buckskin Joe prospecting and acting as Postmaster for the townsfolk. I expect him back by the end of the month."

Then I headed on up to the Printer Boy office and checked in with Judson. The foreman, Cal Jackson had more authority but was generally busy with the mining operation.

My boss, Judson, had been in the gulch for five years and was disgruntled by the fact that a fortune had eluded him and was likely becoming nothing more than a pipe dream. He was grey whiskered, gnarled and stooped, but his attitude toward his fellow man when pressed was moderately amicable.

"Do you have jobs for me, Judson? I'm free to work for a couple days starting tomorrow."

"How's your cabin building coming along, Jasper? Better be about finished or you'll be a racing winter."

He was busy sharpening a knife blade with what I thought of as one of my own personal rasps. Didn't say nothin' though.

"Got the promise of winter snows in the back of my mind,

and that's a fact. It'll take but a week or so to finish up and then the place should be warm and tight enough I reckon."

"Well come on in in the morning. There's three or four drill bits need sharpening and a rod in the crankshaft is wobbly."

"I'll be back here at sunup, then. Judson."

He lifted a hand in a half wave and I was off once again to Doc's where Otis and Sam were awaiting me.

"Hey. You took long enough, Jasper. We already had us a needed whisky and heard us some gossipy news from some of the miners. Let's get in line for grub and we'll tell some tales."

Buster did his thing with the bell clanging.

"Okay, Otis. I'm a 'coming right behind you."

We settled in at our usual table and chatted up with Doc and watched as steaming bowls of stew were set down before us, along with mugs of beer to wash it all down.

"What news, boys? Your cabin coming along alright?"

"Sure is, Doc. A week or so and we'll have a shindig to celebrate the timely construction. You'll always be a welcome guest." I said.

He nodded and was off to make his rounds of the establishment. No mistake why it was a law-abiding place - no gun play. Guns had to be checked at the door.

"So you boys have work on the placers for a few days? I'm planning some smithy work myself before finishing up the cabin. We have hardly any dust left and need supplies to take back over there."

Sam nodded the affirmative and Otis wiped gravy off his mouth before speaking. "Yup. Luck was with us when we spotted Tom Starr in the saloon. Saved us a hike down the Gulch to see him. He gave us the nod to work on some claims in the morning."

We left off gabbing and gave over to eating the savory rabbit stew. Corn bread was good for dunking and wiping up the meaty bits.

"I believe this to be one of the tastiest meals I've had in a month's time." Said Sam.

We nodded our agreement and walked out to the dirt road just as some kind of ruckus or mayhem was starting up down the way in front of the nearly finished fancy house. We stood watching the drama and asked two miners loitering nearby what was up with all the clamor.

These men announced the arrival of a stage carrying five members of the fairer sex. The camp became increasingly noisy and boisterous with wanting a look at the newest cluster of lacquered women.

Soiled Doves Arrive in Oro City

Sam, Otis and me were not in the mindset to pursue this particular pastime. We had a cabin and jobs to take up our time and energy and money. Maybe sometime in the future we would survey the sporting gals but not now.

A freight wagon had rolled along Weston Pass earlier in the week hauling a piano box, and several men were now moving it into a room attached to a saloon a ways down past Tabor's store, maybe a five minute walk from where we stood outside Doc's. So this piano would be the second of two in Oro City.

"Let's walk on down the road and take a gander." I said.

Otis said he didn't mind and Sam never seemed to mind.

We stepped into the saloon smudgy in the dim light. No sunlight from outside, just some lanterns placed here and there along the walls and in back of the bar top. Hard to make out details except the outline of bottles of liquor on wall shelves behind where the barkeep stood.

At the moment Al Smithson, the barkeep, was overseeing the delivery of the newly arrived piano. Its prominent placement next to the side wall would make it visible to passersby on the street.

"Howdy, Mr. Smithson. Could it be possible that one of the French hens new to camp has the ability to play this musical instrument?" Otis asked.

"Not one of those foreign harlots, but I just hired a fair lass who came into camp riding a mare just two days ago. Says she came across the plains with a wagon train some several months before she found her way to Oro City."

"When will she be playing and singing, do you reckon?" I said.

"She's staying in a loft above Tabor's store for the time being. We arranged for a performance in a few days' time. She needs to get her bearings and settle in 'fore she joins the entertainment business. Sure is a comely little thing and sure to be a flourish to this here establishment."

" Ah. Sounds like a good reason to stop by and partake of the entertainment. Thanks." I said.

"I'm ready to find my scratchy pillow for a night's rest. What say you to this, boys?" Said Sam. His speech sounding more and more like his friends.

We complied and headed straight for Doc's and bedding down.

Next day at daybreak we ate a hasty breakfast of flapjacks and molasses and headed out for our provisional jobs. I asked my friends to look in on Pepper before they took off for their placer workings. See if he was still stinking from the skunk.

I found a project that would keep me occupied for the entire day. The foreman, Cal Jackson, needed that same crankshaft worked on again. It required all my attention to get it straightened, but I felt comfortable in my domain and made steady progress.

Many long hours later I was feeling satisfied with my labors and was in a fine mood with a pouch of dust for wages in my boot.

I rounded a bend on my way to meet my buddies and had to step around some men who were inspecting what appeared to be a pile of rags in the road. As I padded by I could see right away that the pile was a man bleeding from a head wound.

"What say we move Joe on down to Tabor's mercantile? See if the Missus might can patch his pate." One of the men said.

I followed behind as the unfortunate man was carried along. I decided to stand around and see what the scuttlebutt was regarding this latest drama.

Come to find out that scoundrel, Charlie Turner, from the big tent camp up yonder between here and our cabin took a shot at Joe who was prospecting above the Printer Boy.

"We got the laws after Turner. He's been a raising cane for far too long and not yet been called to task. This time he's crossed the line. Joe might not make it." Said one of the men.

I walked on so as to check on Pepper to see for myself his state of mind. I never know with my burro. He may still be nursing hurt feelings about the skunk. I walked into his enclosure and greeted him. Holding out a fistful of grain I pointedly approached from the front.

"So you don't smell as vile as you did. The remedy has worked its magic. Think we'll be going back over to the cabin in a few days. You'll do everyone a favor if you use the time to restore yourself. We'll need you to haul a heavy load of supplies for stocking the cabin."

He gave me one of his head jerks. Insufferable.

Then I went in search of Otis and Sam. They were in the saloon which we frequent when in the Gulch.

"You been in here all day, boys?"

"You know better than that, Jasper. We rewashed claims for Starr and he paid us for the day. Should have enough in another day to buy supplies." Said Otis.

"I'm thinking the same. Pour us a whisky, and I'll tell a story which was just developing after I left the Printer Boy."

They waited for me to settle once I had my drink in hand.

And then I relayed the news that Charlie Turner was on the run with a posse on his tail. Poor hapless Joe with a head wound might not survive the night.

We dusted Smithson's palm and walked into the street. Men were still listing about the roadside jawing over the outlaw, Charlie Turner.

"Wouldn't mind seeing that fellow behind bars." Said Otis.

Just then a fellow galloped by announcing loudly that Turner was just brought in wearing irons.

"Y' all come on down to the bottom of the Gulch to witness a lynching party!"

"What say you to this, boys?" I asked my friends.

We hustled along with a dozen others to a site where a

gallows had hurriedly been raised right off the roadway. Five officious looking fellows were climbing stairs to the platform. Sure enough Charlie Turner sneering yet, was just then having a cloth hood pulled over his head.

A tall man with full side whiskers and wearing a black duster spoke to the crowds. He gave the appearance of authority.

"We five men by directive of California Gulch Miners' Law are hereby charged with sending this blackguard to perdition. On the count, men, grab onto the rope."

Before anyone could blink twice the trap door opened and down dropped Turner with a banging clatter. There was heard a collective gasp from the crowd.

Sam and Otis shared a moment of reflection with me as we ambled back up the rutted road toward Doc's and sleep. We would speak of this incident for as long into the future as we remained in one another's company.

Precisely one week later us three were hauling supplies over the hills to our cabin. A burlap bag of dried beans, bucket of lard and thirty pounds of flour were hauled in our makeshift wagon. Pepper's paniers were loaded with the coffee, salt, molasses, matches and candles. Each man had to carry tools and such cook wares as could be procured from various stores. We bought a good iron skillet at Tabor's.

Earlier when working at the cabin we had taken time to nail several shelves to walls for the purpose of keeping our food stuff from up off the dirt floor. We had gotten the boards from a throw-away wagon in the Gulch. Finally, after completing these inside details we dug a cavity into the hill to use for cold storage for game. We nailed some boards to the front so bears and such would not be able to get in.

"All in all I feel satisfied with our efforts. Once the outhouse privy is finished I believe we'll be good and set up." I said.

We had just completed a small enclosure to be used as Pepper's corral.

Along about then Jake appeared in the yard carrying a good sized poke.

"How you boys getting on with your venture? Looks like you got the job done with plenty of days left before the snowy months set in."

"Howdy Jake. Come sit awhile. Sam's just now swept the front area and we're a' thinking to sit and rest ourselves before we tackle the privy. Good sized hole is dug but the walls need to be put together." Otis said.

"Brought you some rabbits I snared just this morning. They'll have to be ate today or go bad. I'll be more than happy to give a hand to putting the finishing labors to your privy."

Good to his word Jake pitched in and we had us a substantial outhouse before the sun had completed its westward path over the yonder mountains.

I helped Jake skin the rabbits while Sam built up a fire in the ring and Otis fashioned a spit. Biscuits baked in the iron skillet and good aromas filled the air all around us that fine afternoon. We even had a small jug of whiskey to pass around. This was a present Doc give us on our last night staying in his boarding house. For a while that is.

"Did you hear what happened the other day over to the Gulch, Jake?"

Got myself settled on a log and went on, "I mean in regards to that blackguard Charlie Turner."

"I haven't left these hills for weeks, so no I haven't heard none of your stories. But let's be out with it, Jasper, before I lose interest and take leave of this refined company."

"Well, you do recollect what a reputation Turner had in all this district here about. By the authority of the Miner's Law committee he found himself dangling from the end of a hangman's noose. Guess you can be an outlaw for only so long before the law catches up to you."

"That's as it should be in this life. You reap what you sow." Said Jake, after taking one last swig from the jug. "I'm off to my cabin and warm bed before the night gets too dark to see by. The full moon will be a lamp but can't be depended on. Plenty of clouds."

"You'd be more than welcome to fix you a pallet on the floor of our cabin and wait till the morrow 'fore you set off." I said.

"Thank you kindly but I need to see after things around my place. Can't leave my property to the woodland critters as we have an understanding that what's mine is mine. Theirs is everything else in the woods. But in my absence no telling how far an unspoken agreement might take all of us."

We waved him farewell and damped down the fire in the

yard ring and decided not to stoke the inside stove. Then we tucked into our new beds and kept warm all night.

Next morning the air had a bite to it as we set about making a fire to boil coffee and rewarm what was left of last night's biscuits.

"Well, boys, this chilly air is a sign of coming fall. Last couple years flurries of snow came along almost as soon as the aspens gold fell to the ground." Said Sam. "What say we take today and stack up some firewood to see us through to spring?"

Nods all around and we set to work sawing, chopping and stacking till we had most of one cabin side covered three layers deep with cut wood. We used a piece of tenting from Otis' original wagon and covered the stacks just in case snow caught us unawares. Then after some jawing back and forth we agreed that a few more days or even a week spent working the placers might be a good idea. So we tidied up around the place, tied a rope onto Pepper and headed out for Oro.

Once more in the Gulch I took my leave and hiked up to the Printer Boy to see if any jobs had availed themselves of my labors. Judson came out of the blacksmith lean to and greeted me with a scowl on his face.

"Hope that look is not because of poorly done work on my part."

"Nah. You should know that your skills are highly commended. My black mood is on account of the same crankshaft you've been repairing off and on. It may be done broke for good this time; a rod is out of alignment and has severely damaged the whole works."

The foreman walked slowly back and forth looking dejected.

"So if you'd take a look I'd be obliged. If it can't be repaired we'll have to send to Denver City for a new one and operations will be shut down in the meantime. Miners will be out of a job and we'll be in a fine pickle."

"If you can send two men over here I'll see what can be done. We'll climb to the top of the stamp mill and dismantle the whole shaft and lower it down here to the forge."

"Consider it done." He said.

And that's what we did. Once the main parts were arranged in the lean-to I set to work straightening the rod on the forge, rolling it round using the steel tongs on the anvil. This took all afternoon and into the shank of the evening but I was satisfied that I could get the apparatus functioning. I put the tools of my trade away and found Judson just locking up the office for the night.

"Think I got it alright. I'll be here first light to finish the job and get it put back up where it does belong."

"I sure do thank you, Jasper. Could I buy you a whisky? I want to see what the newest saloon looks like. Probably no different than any of the others."

"That's mighty neighborly, Judson. I'm expecting to meet up with my partners. We've been storing up wood chunks for the winter out at our cabin."

"That's right. You've been a 'working on that project for some weeks, now. Just about finished with it, are you?"

We were walking along down the road at a good pace. But then paused to look around at all the building going on. Mostly more cabins.

"What would that be then? Five saloons?"

"Yep. And three boarding houses, two supply stores, and a new bath house with rooms upstairs for the sporting women. Not to mention the chippies on The Row in the tented lean-tos." Judson said.

Our first stop was in Golden Creek saloon. We threw down a whisky and headed back outdoors.

Piano music was coming from the very place where we'd seen the musical instrument delivered that morning, Smithson's. There was a crowd of miners standing three deep nudging one another to get inside. They were acting well-behaved, not loud and boisterous, but determined nonetheless.

Just as I spotted Otis and Sam in the horde Judson decided to take his leave. Said he was tired and turned himself towards one of the boarding houses.

I inched my way nearer to my two friends and now could hear a melody being sweetly sung. The tune nudged my memory and whisked me back to the evenings traveling with the wagon train. Could the world produce two identical honeyed voices? Finally abreast of Otis and Sam I pressed them to keep trying for the entrance.

The men were too numerous to push through. One fellow turned to us snarling and looked to be willing to draw us into a fistfight.

"Aw let's just leave it for tonight. Catch the show once the novelty has worn thin. These men will soon lose interest, I reckon." Said Sam.

Otis shrugged and turned to the street, but I was less inclined to give up.

"I know you both will think I'm foolish, but I deeply feel that the delicate voice singing inside is someone I remember from my wagon train days."

"Don't matter much now as we can't even catch a glimpse of her face." Said Otis. "Let's try again some other night."

I was of a mind to set up a camp right there on the dirt walkway in order to check if the voice belonged to the fair Lucinda Poole as I suspected, but my practical mind concurred with the boys. Off we went to Doc's for some sleep.

"Thought you'd been shuck of us, Doc? We surely did enjoy your parting gift of whiskey but will still be needing to stay in your house every now and then. When work keeps us busy of a day here in the Gulch." I said.

Doc gave us the nod.

Next morning just as the sun was creeping over the eastern ridge I sopped the bacon gravy with a small chunk of cornbread and said to Sam and Otis that I'd be an hour or so at the Printer Boy and then we could take off for our new cabin. Then I added, "Would you stop by the corral with a handful of grain for Pepper?"

"Say, Jasper, just whose burro is that sorry animal, anyways? Seems that if it were left to you he'd of starved long ago." Said Otis.

I gave a grunt for an answer and high-tailed it up to the mine.

We met up mid-morning, got hold of Pepper and hiked on up the steep hill and on over the trail to the cabin. The breeze was pleasant and we could smell the pungency of sagebrush and feel dried pine needles crushed under our boots. Wildflowers decorated the slopes right up to the cabin.

I had completely given up the chewing tobacco habit. Couple of reasons – for one, I never really liked the taste of the stuff, and I didn't care for having to search from here to kingdom come when I was down to my last pinch.

Also as we walked along I thought to myself, the small strawberry mark on my face had been fading away as I added years to my age. People didn't hardly remark about it anymore. So all in all fortune was settling in my favor.

At the moment Pepper was snuffling behind me. I turned to regard his visage but saw no reason for his doings.

"Better not be conjuring any shenanigans, my four-footed friend. You're to the point where you have had enough good training and should be able to be counted on."

Otis and Sam were sitting on logs out front of the cabin when the burro and I approached. As Pepper had shown no enthusiasm for bounding quickly along the track, so now my partners had been lounging in the sunshine for some little time.

"What say we take some time to barber one another?" Said Sam.

"I'd be agreeable to that long as I don't end up looking like a skinned varmint."

"Aw could only improve your looks, Otis. For sure that beard has been catching food bits long enough." I said.

So we did just that.

A Fair Songbird

Meantime down in Oro City a pretty young woman was attempting to see herself in a small handheld mirror. Mrs. Tabor most generously provided a loft which had suited, but now with wages in her future it was time to find a more comfortable and permanent lodging. She had just basin-bathed and dressed in a clean grey frock and now meant to go along to several boarding houses before deciding which would be most suitable for her needs.

"I'll be back later to fetch my belongings, Mrs. Tabor. I have enough in my purse to pay for a month and hand you some for your generosity."

"Oh don't go giving all your wages away before you've rooted yourself here in the Gulch. You can pay me at any future time.

Before you are off may I inquire about where exactly you were raised? The reason I ask is that your speech sounds a lot like my long ago home in Maine."

"Oh my goodness! I myself left my family in that exact region. I have felt a certain familiarity with you since we first made our acquaintance. Maine, imagine that!

After this exchange the young woman started down the dusty dirt road. She was wearing her good shoes with buttons along the sides and one inch heels. Her other pair was better for walking but she wanted to look her best today. She had pinned her black curly hair up and wore her newest Denver bonnet. She thought the pinkish color flattering.

Just now she had to jump out of the way of a freight wagon which caused her ankle to twist in the rutted road. The driver paid no heed. He was hauling picks, shovels and such for a new undertaking by two educated miners, Stevens and Woods. It was said that the two men envisioned constructing a ditch for bringing water from the Arkansas River to the placer claims in California Gulch.

After the wagon barreled by, the young maiden limped along a bit but even so managed to pop in and out of three boarding houses while weighing their merits in her mind.

She entered one that looked drab and dreary inside. And immediately her gaze took in the painted face and frilled bodice of a woman sitting somewhat near the entrance. She instantly realized that it was a sporting house and quickly hurried back into the street while silently giving thanks that providence had not made her a participant of such a wretched heart-breaking profession.

A few minutes later she found a building with a suitable façade.

"Hello. I'm searching all around Oro City for favorable accommodations. I have found work playing a piano box in a dancing establishment. Do you have a room you could show me?"

The crusty bewhiskered man to whom she directed her question was sweeping the entrance of a two story building.

"You wouldn't be a harlot making her living on her back, now would you? I'll have none of that sort taking a room here. Won't have it. So tell the truth now because if that fact comes out later you'll soon find yourself on your back in the street."

Lucinda blushed crimson. And tears welled up and threatened to spill over. She inhaled deeply.

"My good man, I assure you that I make my wages by singing and playing the piano box and no other way. My reputation is untarnished. And if a reference is needed please ask the good Mrs. Tabor about me."

"Hmm. Well then I'll show you two rooms and you can take your pick."

She took a moment to look around the small lobby. The room had one embellishment on a single wall. A tiny daguerreotype of a somber woman dressed in severe black. His mother or wife or sister? One could only guess if one cared to take the time. She took the moment to collect a modicum of her lost composure.

Soon she climbed the steep narrow stairs following behind the man. She eventually chose a sunny room with a window looking out over the road. The view took in the opposite wooded hillside with the placer ditch part of the scenery. She had to stand on her tiptoes to get a full look in either direction as she was short in stature, four feet eleven in stocking feet.

"Lodging is two dollars a week. This place is known as The Holiday House. What might your name be, Miss?"

"Lucinda Poole from Maine."

Lucinda had traveled up the Arkansas Valley from the Pike's Peak area. She was weary of moving from place to place with no home to call her own. And so now after procuring the room she walked quickly back to the Tabor store so as to retrieve her belongings.

"I found lodging in Holiday House which seems suitable. I still can't get over the idea that we each called Maine home.

"For now I'd like to purchase some calico for a dress and I'll use the scraps for curtains, Ms. Tabor. The pale background with purple posy print, if you please."

"I have a dress pattern you can use. This fabric will give you sunniness, and I envision you as a lovely decoration in this lackluster place. And indeed curtains always make a room look more cheerful and gay, Miss Poole."

"I was caught off guard and forgot to ask the name of the proprietor of the Holiday House. Would you happen to know?"

"Why that's Frank White's place. He has shown himself to be a smart businessman and runs an above board establishment. He won't cotton to any foolery from scoundrels or cheats or sporting gals. He has a hired hand who keeps riffraff out on the street and away from his boarders. I'm happy to know that you'll be in a safe place."

Lucinda walked back over to the H.H. as she thought to call it in her mind. She took some time to organize her few belongings on the two shelves in her room. The shelves were made from a wooden crate which had been nailed to the wall for the purpose of a cupboard of sorts. The room had a log bedstead complete with a straw mattress and topped with a flimsy coverlet which didn't appear to promise much warmth.

"I'll have to purchase a woolen blanket before the weather turns cold." She thought to herself.

There was a stool and small table against the far wall which she studied and then moved to the window wall. A wash bowl and pitcher she set atop and then laid her precious comb and hand mirror alongside. She removed her bonnet and picked up the mirror and took a few minutes to study her face and hair. Frowning at the gap left when a doctor had pulled a tooth while on the wagon train, she now winced as a twinge of pain came from yet another back tooth opposite the hole.

Sighing Lucinda smoothed her black hair and reworked it into a bun at the nap of her neck. The wisps that framed her face and green eyes looked presentable enough. She pinched her cheeks and chewed on her lips to bring forth some color.

Finally she adjusted her undergarments and brushed off her skirt with a glove before setting out again. She had been taking her meals at a place that served passable fare, a sideline to the lodging, as did most other boarding houses.

Just a few days earlier she'd met the new school teacher, Miss Isabelle Laughlin, and found her company quite pleasing. The young women were of similar age and temperament. So the two had agreed to share a table for meals whenever they chanced to eat at the same time.

The very small place where meals were served was just down the road two buildings from Holiday House. Three bench-es along-side tables in the front and a kitchen in the back. Frank White had said this would be the best place to have her meals.

The school marm was a good four inches taller than Lucinda, very sturdy physically and her warmth of nature glowed from her brown eyes and wide smiling face. Her visage was marred only by her teeth being crowded and somewhat crooked. Her gown was practical and conservative. No fussy lace nor adornments either one.

"Hello, Miss Isabelle. May I join you this evening?"

"That would be such a pleasure, Miss Lucinda. It makes me self-conscious to sit solitary while awaiting my repast. May I inquire about whether you have found more permanent lodgings?"

"It is with a light heart that I might now relate a successful narrative. As of this very afternoon, a Mr. Frank White, proprietor of The Holiday House, and I have struck an arrangement affording me a quite satisfactory room. Mr. White has not been in business long but Mrs. Tabor vouches for him."

"Well that serves as the best of a reference, my dear. I'm quite partial to any advice or recommendation when it comes from that quarter. A four walled chamber attached to the one room school building's far side has proven adequate for my own lodging. And now we have both discovered the same dining establishment."

The teacher covered her mouth with her hand and giggled. A nervous habit, but also an endearing one.

Isabelle then went on, "I am spending considerable time organizing benches for classroom seating. Desks have been on order from the East for months but heaven knows when they might arrive here. My order of slates and readers should come along any day. If the school bell rings before the freight wagon arrives the students will have to make due with two slates and one reader to share. A temporary inconvenience."

A serving man placed bowls of stew in front of them. Biscuits and not so fresh butter were already on the table. A jug of beer was then set down.

"My good fellow, could we forego the beer and have water instead?" A nervous titter followed.

He stopped short and threw a surly look in our direction before stepping on to the next table.

"Well, Isabelle, I think we'll be drinking beer as usual."

"You know, I purchased some cheery fabric today and after I fashion a gown the scraps can be made into curtains for my drab room. I dare say there should be enough left to make some for your classroom, if you'd like."

"Two weeks from yesterday is the first school day, Lucinda, and your suggestion is quite welcome. May we meet on the marrow and work on the classroom window? Or would you prefer to complete your own projects first?"

"Oh there is no urgency to fiddle with my gown and room furnishings. I'm more than agreeable to devise a window design with you and tomorrow would suit just fine after I cut out a dress pattern supplied by Ms. Tabor."

And the two friends, apparently the only reputable young women in camp, save for Augusta Tabor, were most grateful to have one another and so before parting company agreed to meet at the schoolhouse the following day.

Lucinda had been using some of the morning hours each day

to practice playing the dulcimer/piano box as she was far from proficient with it. Also she was gathering a list of all the songs she knew so that when Al Smithson was ready to invite the public to enjoy his venue she would be well prepared.

He had asked her to give him a sample review the other evening but her sweet songs drew crowds of miners into the hall and he'd had to use two of his men to herd them back onto the street. Because of this he asked his singer to manage her practice sessions during morning hours only.

She had a costume of sorts. A maroon velvet bodice fitted over a black satin-like skirt and adorned with a simple paste broach. The fancy type gown was pieced together from some worn out garments that came west with her. She yet longed to have possession of the fine broach that had been made into wedding rings on the wagon train, but all that belonged to yesterday. And today was of course a new day.

The recollection of the rings caused Lucinda musings about the past several months. However, she did not fancy brooding over the heartbreak nor over the difficulties she had had to endure as a wayfarer from Maine. But she often had to forcefully push these thoughts away.

And now finally arriving in this remote inhospitable mountain settlement. She swallowed down tears thinking of the life her young husband had been cheated out of. Additionally, she had not received any correspondence from her people back east which intensified her occasional melancholy and homesickness.

The Cobalt Bottle

By the by, this kind of thinking was simply not to be entertained. She absolutely would not allow her thoughts to be swallowed up by painful memories. Also the mind erasing doses of laudanum. She had once been under the influence of this medication. Her sensibilities had been compromised by overwhelming grief when her new husband suddenly died and so it was that eventually the mind-numbing demon in a bottle became her most unwavering ally.

After spending days and months in a primitive-type sanatorium in Denver City she was granted a miracle in the person of a nurse wearing the habit of the Sisters of Charity of Leavenworth, Kansas. This good woman would not be fazed nor overcome by her mission to combat such addictions. Sister Mary Agnes. She had not been schooled per se in the realm of drug substances. She knew the warning signs because she'd seen the effects and ravages many times before.

So Sister Mary Agnes over saw the care of Lucinda Poole. The nun did not take the laudanum away all at once. Too drastic a therapy could drive a patient over the edge and into madness. But time and a great deal of patience along with smaller doses each day provided noticeable progress. Counseling sessions were part of the treatment and each afternoon Sister would sit with Lucinda and use her wiles to wrest from the girl how she came to her addiction.

The sister was a handsome and agreeable woman of indeterminate age. She had entered the religious life as soon as she reached sixteen, leaving her family's pig farm in Iowa. The Order sent her west to Denver City ten years ago and even though her calling as a missionary to the settlers was sporadic and often ineffective, she was satisfied that her work here was indispensable.

Lucinda would be forever indebted to Sister Mary Agnes for dealing with her drug dependence.

Eventually Lucinda managed to get transport on a stage coach which was bringing folks to this particularly remote mining camp with promise of carving out a hopeful future. As an added thought she reasoned that by sharing her talents life might be more palatable for the men who labored on the placers.

And for the present she felt this endeavor was a worthwhile mission which gave her life some meaning and direction.

The following day around mid-morning the two women, that is Lucinda and Isabelle, met in the school room where they cut and sewed curtains for the solitary window.

After this they took some time to draw out the letters of the alphabet on some whitish paper they procured from a packing crate. With these cutouts they decorated one brown wall. And then the two stood back to admire their handiwork but decided to use the remainder of the paper to draw out numbers and finally pasted these up as well.

"My thanks to you, Lucinda. The students will feel a warm welcome on the first school day because you took time to make their classroom so inviting."

"No need to thank me, Isabelle. I am just so happy that we are friends. The winter will not be so burdensome with your companionship to carry me throughout the cold and snowy months."

Later on Lucinda walked down the dusty rutted road to Al Smithson's dance hall. Her ankle was no longer sore but just now her tooth was making her miserable. Well no matter, for the present she must remember to order boots for the winter at the Tabor store. And sooner rather than later.

She greeted her new boss as she entered the place. Truthfully she thought him no different than any other fellow hereabouts in dress and visage. He sported bushy side whiskers and plentiful dark hair under his grimy bowler. Medium height, which meant that Lucinda must look up to meet his gaze.

His manner was all business. Any means by which to make money from happenstance was the motivation that drove his pursuits. And the fair Lucinda was much more than happenstance. She was his guarantee that income would soon be forthcoming and plenteous.

Therefore Smithson was already mentally counting the gold dust that his new singer would likely be generating from each performance. And so he behaved with Lucinda as with one who was in high favor. With diffidence so as to retain her for a long spell. He wanted her happy and content. He would see to it that the dance hall patrons showed her the highest respect. Thereby guaranteeing that no one would ever get the idea that she was one of the soiled doves from the row or the brothels.

Lucinda tried finding the piano keys to match her melody.

It was very frustrating and time consuming. But she nevertheless persevered.

After a particularly discouraging session she sighed deeply and walked out into the cloudy late morning. The hem of her skirt seemed to perpetually collect dust from the road and so she kept bunching the dress in her fists and shaking the dirt off as she strode along in the direction of the schoolhouse located up beyond the Tabor store.

Miners were out and about their business and as she walked one or two doffed their hats. She gave them a modest chin tilt. No smile. No chance of them misinterpreting her comportment. She turned into Tabor's store with heavy boots and wool blanket in mind.

"Hello, my dear. How is everything progressing for you?"

"Hello, Mrs. Tabor. Actually after twisting my ankle the other day, I have determined to order some sturdy boots before the winter sets in. I have a second pair of shoes but neither will be suitable for snow and mud. Do you have any in stock today?"

"None but large sizes that would never fit your small feet, I'm afraid. But I will gladly add your request to my list here. When the freight driver comes by I'll tell him to search the stores in Denver City. You won't care that fashion is not a factor. Practicality is what will matter to you once the snow begins to pile up in this gulch. Here, let me measure your foot."

"Thank you for your welcome attention to me."

"You have become a favorite with me, Miss Poole. Are you going to begin entertaining folks in Al Smithson's Hall one of these days soon? I would like to come and support your variety of entertainment. Goodness knows we are sorely lacking in any type of decent pastime."

"I have been rehearsing my music quite ardently of late. As soon as I have conquered the pianoforte to my satisfaction I will begin to entertain on a regular schedule. I should think that it will not be longer than a few more days."

"Well I'm delighted and promise to come to Mr. Smithson's establishment to attend your performances.

"Check back with me in two or three weeks regarding your boots order. You may take this heavy blanket with you now if it suits."

"Thank you, Ms. Tabor. Please set the blanket aside for me and I'll collect it when the boots arrive."

Lucinda decided to go back to her room to rest before tackling another session of practice at the Hall. Once inside she dipped a hanky in the water bowl on the bench and rubbed it vigorously over her teeth. It was one of her back molars that was aching and she knew the time must come to have it extracted. Hopefully very soon.

On her walk she happened to glance down the road at the noisy construction of the newest fancy house. It was a two story building across the road from where she and Isabelle ate their meals. She noticed a galvanized steel tub in the yard that looked to be japanned and realized that this structure's purpose was for men laying up with women of the half world but also would be offering baths as well.

Lucinda thought that bathing was always a necessity and should not be a luxury. And well she remembered the days on the way west when the only time she properly bathed was at a river crossing. But at those times she had to enter the water without disrobing. The only other way to rid herself of the trail's mucky dust and dirt would be to avail herself of a bucket while crouching behind a blanket hung from a wagon to give some degree of privacy. And scrub away.

Her thoughts still on the sporting house made her determined to take her business to a bathhouse situated in one of the conventional boarding establishments tomorrow or at least before the first evening of work.

She went to her room now to rest her mind and quiet her anxieties.

It was late afternoon and she looked out her window to where the creek sparkled and foamed and spotted Isabelle walking along. She tied on her bonnet and draped a shawl around her shoulders then hurried to meet her friend.

"Hello, Lucinda. Are you joining me for supper this evening?"

"Why yes, I am. But I hoped to show you the hall and musical box that has been taking up so much of my time before we go for our dinner."

Isabelle was agreeable to Lucinda's suggestion and so they went directly to Smithson's Hall. The proprietor was within arranging some benches and rustic tables some of which had once been part of wagons. The place was quite drafty because it hadn't yet been winterized by calk or mortar.

"Here we are, Isabelle. May I offer a brief presentation?"

"Please do. I am filled with a heightened curiosity."

Lucinda sat on a stool which had been hewn from a stout tree stump and covered with some straw filled burlap. She fingered the few keys that she had already discovered and hoped would assist with most melodies and now began to sing "In the Sweet By and By".

"Oh, I remember hearing that hymn in our small country church when I was barely just out of pigtails."

"I'm afraid I have a limited repertoire and aside from a handful of gospel tunes I know only a few folksy songs taught me by my grandmother."

"Anyone would be thrilled to come listen to your sweet voice. I mean to say that you are exceedingly talented. But you must have been told this time and again."

Lucinda sighed and then lightly laughed. "Not once have I heard such lovely compliments. No one on the wagon train bothered to say anything other than nodding in time to my music. Of course we were always so burdened by heavy circumstances and exhaustion that none seemed to have energy for kindly words."

As the two were walking the short distance to supper a lavishly lacquered woman sashayed along down the road. Her gown was full skirted with rows of flounces and the bodice had a most revealing neckline. Her beribboned bonnet did not quite cover her curls, the color of which looked unnatural. Henna dye had been applied to her head and appeared too orange. And also, her costume was wholly frivolous and impractical for this place. All of which emphasized exactly what her profession was in Oro City.

In fact there was no doubt what this sort did to earn a living.

And many asserted that their income was substantial. Hens on the row often made better wages than the miners.

But an upstanding female's reputation was to be prized at all costs. So Isabelle and Lucinda averted their gazes even though they were mightily curious to study the woman's fancy garments.

A bird was tweeting sweetly in a pine tree next to the hall.

"Isabelle, why don't we walk into the woods and pick wild raspberries one day soon?"

"Oh, what a lovely idea. I'd love to."

Entering what they called "the hall" they saw that they would be served rabbit stew and brown bread once again for this supper. Meals were a bit tedious but because in past times they had known hunger time and again they did not complain but rather bowed heads in thanksgiving.

Lucinda awoke the next morning with a homesick feeling for her family left behind in Maine. Her younger brothers were noisy and rambunctious and her ma and pa always laboring on a piece of farmland that seemed stingy with its yield. Barely enough to survive on. Nevertheless, Lucinda missed the home she'd left several months ago. She sighed deeply and scolded herself for this moment of downheartedness.

The rent she paid for her room included the emptying of a bed pan and the refilling of her wash basin. She now answered a knock and allowed entry to a young boy, Joe, so that he could undertake these tasks.

Lucinda grimaced as she looked into her hand mirror. Her face was noticeably swollen. The sore tooth was causing her untold misery on this day which probably was the foremost reason for her overall moodiness.

"Say, Joe, is there a dentist in the Gulch who might minister to an ailing patient?"

Joe was grimed from head to toe because of his daily chores but never gave a thought to spending good wages for bathing. The natural color of his hair could only be imagined.

"Well, Miss. The blacksmith will get you out of trouble from a rotten tooth. Cause there ain't no dentist in these parts."

"But where might I find such a worthy person who practices this trade?"

"Just the smithy up at the Printer Boy. He should be found at his forge most days. Least ways that's been the talk around. He's a real pip smithy by most accounts."

"Hmm. Well thank you for this good information. Say, will you be attending Miss Isabelle's school when she opens the doors next week?"

"Not me, Miss. I have jobs to do that keeps me mam and me sisters from the poor house. Me pa died last winter during a blizzard. He got lost in a drift and wasn't found for a month. Now it's all up to me; and I can't give up any time just for reading and writing and ciphering. They ain't of no use to me in such a place as this be."

After this speech Joe turned away and carefully planted each foot on one stair after another so as to keep the boots that were obviously too large for his feet from slipping off. These boots had been worn by his father and now would be the boy's only legacy.

Lucinda set out to inquire about the smithy. As was commonly her first choice when needing counsel Augusta Tabor's store was this day's destination.

"Good morning, my dear. I have been wondering how you've been faring these mild summer days. The weather has been so agreeable of late that one finds harsh winter storms hard to imagine. Although we know cold and snow are likely just around the corner. And as sure as time marches on the seasons will change."

"Really, Ma'am? Not so soon as all that, I pray."

She could still clearly recollect the blowing snow and howling wind which made her way west all that much more miserable. Two young mites still in diapers died of croup just days apart. Each was buried a dozen steps away from the wagon ruts.

"Mrs. Tabor, do you know of a smithy up at the Printer Boy who has skills to relieve a person of a rotten tooth?"

"Yes. I have encountered the young man and his partners a few times this past spring. He stops in here when in need of small tools and such. I can't recall his name but I will wager that he is upstanding in ways of dealing with folks. He appears to be quite principled.

Why do you inquire of him? Do you have torment from a toothache?"

"Oh, my yes! It is an agony that will not leave me with a

moment of peace."

"Well, be off with you on up to the Printer Boy. And best of luck."

"Thank you, Mrs. Tabor. You are a solace to me."

Lucinda stepped out into the road just as a freight wagon pulled up to the store's entrance. She had to jump out of the way of the team of mules.

"Beg pardon, Miss. My mules lack manners." The bewhiskered mule skinner called down to her from his perch. He then spat a stream of tobacco juice onto the road before shrieking and cussing to his mule team.

The young woman dipped her chin in acknowledgement and walked briskly along the road towards her boarding house. She lacked the pluck to face a painful extraction at the moment. She thought she would ask Isabelle to accompany her in the morning. Boost her resolve.

After an attempt at napping Lucinda took out her calico and spent the remainder of the afternoon sewing on her day gown. She sat by the window to give herself added light.

Later that same evening when the two friends met for supper Lucinda mentioned the idea of looking for raspberries in the hills. Isabelle embraced the plan.

"Thorny vines dripping with berries, oh what a lovely way to spend a morning. I haven't thought to do something like this since I've been in Oro City."

"Lovely indeed. But aside from this pleasure I must undertake something most disagreeable. So you see my reverie of berry picking is meant to buoy my spirit so that then I will go forth to face the inevitable episode."

"Tell me of this loathsome experience you are facing, Lucinda."

"Oh. I fear I'm being overly dramatic. My tooth is causing me pain and torment. But because Oro has no dentist I must contact the blacksmith up at the Printer Boy. Hopefully he will be able to perform the extraction. Mrs. Tabor had a single clove which she said might ease the pain some if I could keep it on the offending tooth. It is not helping, though.

But, Isabelle, let us use the morrow for berry picking and then the following day hopefully you could accompany me to the mine's forge."

So, it was decided. Fun and then anguish.

Although the next morning started out overcast, by the time the women met the clouds were burning off and a blue, blue sky was showing through.

They wore their oldest worn out clothes and each tucked the ends of their dresses under the skirt waist so that legs could be freed for hiking.

Angling along an upslope to the trees on top of the hill was easily managed. Once they climbed that far they turned and looked back down and saw the cabins and buildings along the road with a novel perspective.

"Look at the new gambling hall. Seems to have been built entirely overnight."

"Mr. Smithson will have plenty of competition from that quarter. I am going to suggest that he has me singing in no more than three days' time. Just as soon as I can get my tooth seen to."

After this brief exchange they set off once more. The goal was to climb all the way to the topmost incline. They had a notion that the berries would present themselves beside the aspens. And they were right.

Lucinda spotted the bushes with red tinged leaves on thorny vines and sat herself down on a protruding rock. She fanned her face with her bonnet but soon replaced it. Protection from the sun was always a necessary consideration.

They both ate the first berries they picked before dropping some into a small pail. The pail came from the school room to be used for holding pieces of chalk. The chalk was for tomorrow. The fruit was occupying them for today.

They were happy and laughing about any silly thing that popped into their heads. Bees were buzzing around and two small chipmunks played a game of chase around the nearby pine trees. The breezes were so gentle and the day so fine that even with a brimming pail they dawdled before setting off down into the Gulch once more.

Meeting early the next morning they delivered the berries to the cook at the hall where they took their meals. He made flapjacks and sprinkled them generously with the fruit. It was a tasty treat.

Afterwards they met again on the dusty road just before noontime.

The morning had been busy with sewing and tidying up her

room, but Lucinda had been constantly distracted by her toothache. Now she turned to her friend.

"Well I am of two minds about this smithy treating my ailment. On the one hand I can barely keep myself from hastening to him, but on the other hand I keep thinking that his grimy trade is no place to turn for a remedy."

To take her friend's mind off the inescapable affair Isabelle was chattering about a young boy who was to be her student.

"His name is Alfred and under all the freckles there must be a face. His dad is a mule skinner and his mother has three more youngsters to care for, all younger than Alfred.

It must be so tiring and tedious to have to face each day with a husband who's rarely home to lend a hand."

"I imagine the lad will have numerous chores to take care of before he enters the school room. And more of the same at the end of the school day.

"The boy Joe who takes care of chores at my place will not be able to attend school at all for these same reasons."

"Yes. Well I suppose that endless work is all part of life in a mining camp. Toil into the late afternoons and face a new morning with the same chores to complete even before the school bell beckons again."

"And here we are at the Printer Boy. Those stairs lead to the mine office. Guess we might inquire about the smithy up there." And so skirts in hand the young women climbed the stairs.

Jasper and Lucinda Meet Again

Me, Sam, and Otis had been putting in full demanding days at our jobs in the Gulch. Sam and Otis continued to rewash Tom Starr's placer claims with some fairly decent results. Just last week for instance after the dust was weighed and added up, $67.00 was totaled. Mr. Starr was pleased and told the boys that they could expect to be in his employ until the snows made the activity impossible. Another two months or so, he reckoned.

Early each day I could be found working the forge at the Printer Boy. I was content and gratified with the labor. None of the jobs taxed me beyond my abilities. Every once in a while I had to figure a way to go about a task but if I took time to study the undertaking I was rewarded with success.

Men in the Gulch found me of a pleasant nature and my attitude agreeable and helpful. Beside these attributes they felt my work was always top notch.

Pepper had been stabled in the same corral for all these summer months. He seemed to be a favorite with any person who had a fondness of animals. This was cause for amusement albeit baffling, as Pepper continued to give me a run for my money on a regular basis.

Master and beast sometimes shared a meeting of the minds but this did not always include a healthy respect for what each expected from the other.

On this fine summer day I held a handful of grain under the

burro's chin. Pepper nuzzled the breakfast with relish.

"I s'pose some exercise would be in your near future. I'll be back around for you later on this afternoon. We'll go on a rabbit hunt."

Pepper whinnied and as I turned to leave the burro gave my arm a nudge.

"Hi ho, you little fiend."

I set off over to the Printer Boy.

The roadway was dusty and dry as always. This would turn to frozen mud with the first snows. But for now everyone seemed to enjoy the season of blue, blue skies and soft pleasing breezes. Birds showed their gratitude in song and there seemed to be a particular quietude all around.

Having tied my heavy leather apron around my waist I then took a quick inventory of the tools and implements at my disposal.

The mine foreman Jackson came in briefly to check that I was aware of the week's jobs.

"There was a fair lass in here yesterday whiles you was up to your cabin, Jasper. Said she has need of your services. I wouldn't know how you might be of service, but she seemed in a desperate state."

"What did she say was her need, Cal?"

"A toothache."

"Well I have never executed such an assist. Don't know how I'd go about such as this. How'd the girl figure to bring her malady my way?"

"Said Mrs. Tabor sent her to your lair, Jasper. No dentist in the Gulch so your smithy skills is the only other means."

"Hmm. Well I best be looking over my set of pliers so's I can give them a good sanitizing in case she shows up here again. Makes me a mite nervous, I'll admit."

"Let me know how it turns out and best of luck to you."

And so I was left to school myself on dentistry.

I began by lining up the various sizes and shapes of pliers. Picking up the smallest of these which had a needle nose I took a rough rag and attempted to clean black soot and creosote from the business end. To no avail. I chose a rasp and moved it back and forth over the pliers. This worked better but taking yet another rag I rubbed and could see that the tool still appeared not particularly clean.

I sat back on my stool and ruminated. Then I rasped again.

I was far from satisfied but felt my efforts were just as near to resulting in cleanness as I was to procure for this day. I tidied up and left to meet my friends.

"What do you know, Otis? Sam? I'm hungry enough to eat a bear. Don't know why. I haven't been doing work that takes muscle or energy."

"Hi ya, Jasper! We did our part finding color in the creeks

today. Went up to Tabor's store and the Missus weighed it. Nine dollars. Guess we'll have enough for a whisky after supper and then plenty for stocking up on supplies for the cabin. Folks say you can't overdo on stocking up so as to stretch goods to last throughout one of these high mountain winters."

Sam added, "We've been aggravated by the heavy black sand as usual. We could work thrice as fast without that ol' stuff getting in the way, and that's a known fact."

As we went into the boarding house we spotted the landlord Doc walking over to us.

"Howdy, boys. What say you as to news?"

"No news as such, but here's a nut. I'm to be in the dentistry business come the morrow." And saying it out loud I turned to face my friends so's to note their reactions.

"What's this you say, Jasper?" Asked Otis as he took a seat at the supper table.

"It's the truth. Mrs. Tabor has told it here and about that I am the man to see when a tooth is causing misery. Seems she sent a young lady up to the Printer Boy while we were at the cabin last few days. Looking for me to be her savior. Could go either way."

"Cook's got venison stew and cornbread tonight. I'll be glad to join you at the saloon after the men have eaten."

"Sounds fine, Doc. We'll meet you there." Said Sam as he sat down next to me and Otis.

We nodded to Doc and then the three of us ate with no further talking. Stories could wait until we were relaxing in the saloon.

The night was soft and just a little muggy which could portend rain. The thin air was usually very dry in these hills, so a moistness was an easy predictor of any weather change.

We entered the saloon and ordered whisky and before long Doc came in and joined us. He had a trimmed beard and neckline. Noticeable to the others.

"I just heard yesterday that a certain Reverend Robinson, friend of Tom Starr, has been restoring an abandoned saloon down at the bottom to use as a chapel. Talk is that services will be held there in a few weeks, maybe sooner."

"You don't say, Doc! That is news and welcome far as I'm concerned."

Otis tipped his head back and drained his whisky shot as he spoke. We both nodded in unison.

The talk was centered around placer reworks and religious meetings, and to my chagrin japes about sore teeth.

I was quiet and allowed a memory of a very young widow from the wagon train to slip into my mind. I didn't dwell on the past as a rule. Most everyday happenings were more than enough to keep my thoughts from straying in directions of no practical use. Whimsy.

The saloon was thick with cigar smoke and boisterous miners slaking their thirst with whisky. A fight was brewing near the door and the barkeep went in that direction so's to push the rowdies out into the street. This was a common occurrence and drew no notice from the other patrons. Savvy ones would hastily duck out of the way when there was gunplay, though.

With a profound sigh I turned to my friends and stepped away from the bar.

"I'm a' going out to see after Pepper and then likely turn in. I can't keep my mind from worrying over tomorrow and what I'll be facing with this tooth business."

Otis spoke for our group. "I'm guessing the whole thing might be unnecessary if by chance the lass recants and foregoes the procedure."

"Well that would be the best outcome, but not too likely if she indeed has a tooth paining her every minute. Care to walk along to the corral?"

Otis said he'd accompany me, his friend but Sam declined as he was still nursing a whisky.

So we two walked into the night. As we moved toward the corral I removed my hat and slapped it smartly against my leg, a puff of dust floated off.

Admittedly I had a tendency to converse with my four legged companion. Mentally, Otis snorted and grinned at his friend's indulgences with Pepper.

"Here you go, burro. I'll just empty the bucket as the grain is nearly to the bottom. I see you've got plenty of water left. Day after next we'll be heading on up to the cabin with supplies so there's an enjoyable outing you can be sure to count on in your near future."

Carrying the bucket to the outer side of the enclosure and leaving it for the morrow me and Otis then ambled back to the boarding house and sleep. As for me, though, a restless night while thinking about what awaits me in the morning.

The sun did rise on schedule in Oro City. I drank my coffee and ate a breakfast of flapjacks with molasses before starting off up the rutted road toward the Printer Boy.

Lucinda dressed in her calico, pressed her bonnet down which flattened the topmost curls and then glanced into her hand mirror. Her cheek was swollen and the throbbing tooth had not abated in tormenting her. She would not have breakfast for what was the point? She could not chew.

As she set off she wished that Isabelle was accompanying her to the smithy, instead of getting the classroom ready, but inwardly she told herself that she could brave the experience on her own. Now though, she regretted her foolhardy certitude.

As she walked along her mind was filled with trepidation. Her insides fluttered with anxiety.

Meantime, while frowning at my unsightly pliers, I slipped on my apron and stood in the shadowed entrance of the forge. From this vantage point I could see about a quarter way down the length of the Gulch. Many of the placers were being worked and a freight wagon had just pulled up to the Tabor storefront.

The sun was warming the morning and a jay was squawking to its mate in a pine tree over my right shoulder. For the moment I closed my eyes as contentment and reverie were the morning's benediction. My German words often assisted me with mental visuals.

"Hello. Are you the Printer Boy smithy?"

My head snapped around in the direction of the voice and I squinted into the sun. I then shook my head to clear the cobwebs and drew in a deep breath. I was seeing a vision and my brain told me it could not be real. I just stared wide-eyed for a number of seconds.

"That be me, Ma'am." Silently I scolded myself, "Idiot. Get hold of yourself."

"Sir, I am in desperate need of your services. You see, my tooth is quite poorly. I am told that you are schooled in dentistry."

"Well, not schooled as such. But I have mastery of smithy tools and should be able to offer my services in an emergency."

The vision nodded.

"Come hither and I'll have a look-see." I had her sit on a bench just outside the entrance and asked that she open her mouth wide. Peering inside I could see the discolored offender. I took some minutes to assess it.

She thought to untie the ribbons of her bonnet and lay it to the side.

Now taking a whisky bottle from a shelf inside the forge I poured a generous measure into a jar I had at hand.

"Here. Drink this all down. It will afford a numbing effect and spare you some from the pain."

The fair maiden did so, as she appeared to know that she could tolerate no further tortuous agony. She gagged and coughed but managed to empty the jar.

"Here now, sit for some minutes so's to give the medicine time to work."

I thrashed about mentally, and could not keep my eyes from scrutinizing her features. "Yes," I thought, "this is the lovely young lady from the wagon train. It can be no other."

She seemed not to have any recognition of me. However, because the girl was swaying from side to side on her bench, and then hiccupping and giggling a bit, she was cognizant of nothing.

"Okay, Miss. I'll just fetch my implement and endeavor to relieve you of your misery."

I quickly ducked back inside and reappeared momentarily with pliers in hand. Over my arm I'd draped a rather grayish half-clean rag.

"Now you must try to open your mouth as wide as possible."

Nervously perspiring, I grasped her jaw with my left hand, peered inside her mouth and guided my pliers onto the tooth. Drawing in a deep breath I gave a mighty yank and out flew the rotten tooth onto the ground.

Well, at this, everything seemed to happen at once. The woman shrieked, fell forward and fainted into my outstretched arms. I snatched the rag from my arm and attempted to catch the blood flowing from her mouth. Some of it reddened her bodice but I kept the dingy cloth near her mouth for some minutes while holding onto her tightly to keep her from tumbling onto the ground to where the tooth had rolled.

After several minutes she began to display some animation and quivered a bit. Still quite groggy from the whisky she swayed sluggishly in my solid arms.

I did not mind the time it was taking for her to come around. In fact the better part of a half hour had passed before she was able to respond to me. I'd been unabashedly studying each of her facial characteristics. Her soft pink cheeks, her dark curls, a nose that turned up ever so slightly at the tip, thick eyelashes from eyes closed now in repose.

I was beguiled.

Eventually Lucinda struggled to sit up properly and attempted mightily to focus her thoughts.

"I don't like to send you off in such a state. In fact I have determined to hold onto you while walking you to your rooms."

"No, Sir, do not trouble yourself. I am quite able to get to my place without further troubling you."

The next minute she was staggering to her feet. But she held onto my arm to steady herself.

"I insist, Madam. Take care to hold tightly to my arm. I will wrap my other arm around you as we move along."

Lucinda was in no condition to argue and so allowed me to guide her down the always dusty road which at the moment was providentially void of wagons and swiftly galloping horses.

"Which building is your domicile?" My words sounded wooden to me.

"It is called the Holiday House nearby Mrs. Tabor's store."

Her words were slurred and sluggishly spoken. Her feet shuffled alongside her guide.

As we passed the schoolhouse Isabelle was just walking into the street. She rushed to her friend who appeared to be under much duress.

"My good man, I shall take my friend in hand. You have done quite enough. It seems she is under the unfortunate influence of spirits!"

"Well, Madam, it was the tooth extraction which necessitated giving her whiskey to deaden the pain of the ministration. I might add that without strong drink she would have had to endure extreme agony."

"If I have misspoken I do apologize. I did not realize the full extent of the situation before jumping to an injudicious conclusion. Nevertheless, I believe it prudent that now I myself help my friend up to her room. Your further assistance will not be necessary."

"Well then I wish a good day to you both." And doffing my hat I turned and walked away.

Isabelle guided Lucinda slowly up the stairs to her room. She then helped her friend into a lying position on the bed, removed the top portion of her garment and said, "This bodice must be soaked in cold water immediately or the stain will set."

Isabelle lifted the pitcher and found it empty. So she hurried down to the creek and filled it. After returning to the room she filled the basin and dropped the stained piece in. For some minutes while Lucinda rested she swished and scrubbed at the calico. Then she wrung it out tightly, shook out the wrinkles and spread it out on the shelf.

"There. I believe your garment will be good as new when it has dried."

"Thank you. Did you see him? My savior? I can feel pain no more where the tooth was. I will always hold the smithy in high regard for freeing me of the offending tooth."

"Yes of course I saw the man. He was holding you quite tightly when I came upon the two of you. At first I admonished him for giving you spirits, but then checked my indignation as I more fully comprehended the circumstances."

"Oh my. I had been in such distress for so overlong a time. My tooth was hurling me down into the depths of despair. I absolutely owe the fellow my most exceedingly heartfelt gratitude."

"He seemed a sensitive type. Quite solicitous regarding your well-being. His attire was that of a working man, but he seemed clean about his person. I can impart no negative traits whatever."

"Isabelle, you sound as though you wanted to find him lacking in comportment. I pray you will be more generous with your forthcoming feelings toward him."

"Oh! I was thinking only of you, especially the idea that malicious gossip might follow if someone passing were to misconstrue what they thought they saw. You must know that I am your loyal friend always." She clasped her friend's hands in her own and pressed them to her bosom.

"I do know this and of course I do appreciate your guarding my reputation. But tell me more of his physical features. Please."

And Isabelle related what she could recall from the brief encounter.

"He was clean shaven, dark hair under a floppy hat, not tall nor short, and a pleasing visage. Forgive me. I was in a heated state when I happened upon you on the road, so I did not take careful stock of his appearance. However, he did place you most chivalrously into my care before leaving us."

Now saying that she had work at the schoolhouse Isabelle then took her leave.

Lucinda thought to herself, "Well, when I am feeling up to it I will take a walk up to his shop and thank him properly. I only wish I had the means to bake him a cake or muffins."

She then happened to look into her small purse and noted the coins within.

"Oh no. I failed to give the man payment for his services. I must see after this omission at the most proximate time. He must think me extremely lacking in manners, moreover ungracious and boorish."

Before long she napped.

When she awoke she took note of her condition by moving her tongue around the inside of her mouth and immediately felt the hole. Gratitude flooded her mind and she again thought to hasten to the forge in order to render payment within the hour.

But peering out the window she noticed rain coming down in torrents turning the roadway into a mire of mud and offal.

She lingered there at the window for some minutes enjoying the downpour and the freshness of the air. In time her thoughts returned to the happenings of the day and she attempted to recall what she could of the smithy and of his willingness to take matters of dentistry into his own hands. He easily might have refused such a curious undertaking.

But he did not.

The day had seamlessly turned into dusk and the rain did not abate.

I ran through the storm as thunder and lightning erupted in earnest. Rounding the side of the corral I stopped short. Pepper was gone. I felt panic along with a huge expanse of exasperation, although I did not instantly react to it. Rather I breathed in and out deeply. Okay. Where to begin looking.

I thought to involve my buddies in a search. Running through puddles of water and sloppy mud, I ducked into Doc's.

A serving lad was loitering within and I asked, "Have you seen Otis and Sam this evening?"

"Who you say?"

"Never mind. I think I see them now racing through the downpour."

I darted into the road and nearly ran Sam over in my haste.

"What the…"

"Sorry, Sam. I need you both urgently. Pepper is missing."

"Queer. I noticed that you had him hobbled properly last night. So how did the beast get loose?"

"I'll worry on that later. Would you boys look along the creek while I climb the hillside?"

Agreement all around.

An hour later I still hadn't found the burro, so I set off back down into the Gulch.

Before long what do you know? Here came my pals leading Pepper along.

Approaching them at a trot I had to raise my voice over the noise of the storm. "Why, where did you finally capture him?"

Otis jerked on the rope and handed it over to me.

"He had tucked into one of Tom Starr's out buildings and was helping himself to a bucket of grain. Hadn't been in there long enough for Tom to take notice. It was just by chance that we saw him. To get out of the storm we were of a mind to dry off ourselves in that barn and there he was."

I shook my head as I led Pepper back to his corral. The rain was now just a drizzle.

"See you boys at Doc's shortly."

And to the burro, "Don't know as I can rightly blame you for bolting during the noise of a storm. What I can't figure out is how you got free of the rope-hobble. You don't need no more feed as I was told that you stuffed yourself down at Starr's."

I treated my friends to a double whiskey after dinner to repay them for their help. We made plans to use the morrow to stock up on supplies as we were counting on getting back to the cabin before the week ended.

At breakfast we all lingered over our coffee for once as we had no need to rush to our jobs. We felt we needed to take a detailed mental inventory of any items yet to procure because we agreed that in a month or less we would not be making regular runs from the cabin into the Gulch.

I remained seated at the table after Otis and Sam said they'd be going on ahead to Tabor's store. I rested my chin in my palm as my head was yet full of Lucinda Poole. I mused about the fact that the young lady was right here in California Gulch. Now what were the odds of that happening? I pondered over how she chose to come to this particular place when she could have traveled to so many others in the west.

Sighing, I shook my head remembering yesterday - pulling the bad tooth, holding her in my arms and studying her fair face for such a long and extended period of time. I recalled so many details about her. Her dress, plain but pretty, her hair stuck in wisps around her face, her mouth a perfect bow, and of course the weight of her as I held her in my arms.

I felt that I could live on these memories for the rest of my earthly life.

Living was full of surprises. Some welcome and some not so much.

But for now I needed to get over to the store and join my friends.

I approached the men as they were hefting bundles into the makeshift wagon. Sam was sitting next to the storefront lacing up a new pair of boots.

"Nice boots, Sam. Been waiting for them a spell, I recollect."

He grunted an affirmation.

"Got here in a nick of time. We were just a' thinking how we'd like to do the whole job before you'd show up to help. That way you could save your strength for when you next have to chase down that poor excuse of a burro." Otis wiped his forehead with a rag from his pocket. And spit into the dirt.

"That's why I shuffled along enjoying the fine day. And thanks to you for considering my sensibilities."

I liked my friends for this joking manner even if at my own expense. My brother Horst used to play with me like this, and memories of home were always welcome. I never received letters. But I vowed to write one to my folks and hand it to the good Father Dyer whenever the man walked over into Oro City again.

"Look what we have here in the wagon cart. Some cans of peaches! On a snowy day at the cabin fruit will be a most welcome treat." Sam said this as he swung the leather strap over his shoulder.

"Looks like you've volunteered to pull the wagon up to the rented mule, eh?"

"Might need some help from you, as you well know, Jasper. Let's get moving 'fore we've wasted another full day of sunlight."

The three of us made good time hiking over the hills to our sturdy cabin. It took way longer than an hour to get there when we were hauling supplies.

Pepper was actually carrying his share today and seemed to be enjoying the woods. Two blue jays were swooping and looping in a joyful dance. The burro swayed his head back and forth as if he were joining the birds in their happiness. The breezes seemed to kiss each aspen leaf which gave the trees the appearance of quaking.

Each of us did a quick inspection of the surroundings as we approached the cabin. Something wasn't quite right. The earth was disturbed in the yard and much more so around the door.

None of us fellows had a firearm handy. Two rifles had been left in the cabin for hunting, because not one of us would be of a mind to use a gun except under the direst of circumstances. We were not in the habit of carrying a gun.

"What say you, Otis? Sam? Should we charge through the door so as to catch the culprit red-handed?"

"Shush. Listen. Do you hear a rustling within?" This from Sam who had dropped his goods next to the mule and was creeping closer to the door.

At this moment Otis stormed forward and threw his bulk against the door which flew open into the interior.

Several sets of glowing eyes stared at us. Surely they were the rightful inhabitants and the men the intruders.

Raccoons!

What a ruckus ensued as the bandits hissed and stood their

ground. Sam grabbed a stout branch from a nearby evergreen and whacked at the critters but had negligible luck.

Otis and me did likewise and before long our joint forces were able to rid the cabin of all the coons. A family of five.

An inspection of the interior revealed that we had interrupted an assault on our stores of foodstuffs. Cornmeal and dried beans coated the floor around to the shelves.

"I feel duped by the critters. Look up here. The chimney offered an open invitation to them. If we hadn't come back when we did they might have eaten up the whole shebang." I said as I began sweeping up the mess.

"Lucky the raccoons didn't invite a family of bears to join the feast." Otis said, as he walked out to unload the panniers from off the mule and burro.

Sam swallowed hard and flinched. "Bears?"

"Yep. The bears are using the last of summer days to fatten up before hibernating. You know this, Sam, don't you?"

"Yes, I reckon I do, Jasper. But I don't like to imagine them sharing my sleeping quarters."

"I'm thinking of making a quick hike up to Jake's cabin. See if he knows any tricks to covering the chimney hole so's critters can't get into the place again. You boys think you might take the afternoon and hunt some game? We could smoke and dry the meat tomorrow and be that much further ahead of the winter snows."

The three of us agreed on the plans and went about preparations to make it all happen.

As I hiked up the steep hill to my friend's cabin my head was full of figuring how to keep critters out of the chimney. I supposed I could make an apparatus of some kind over at the forge.

"Hi ho the cabin!" I hollered as I approached.

Jake came ambling into the yard from somewheres at the back of the structure.

"What say you, my friend? I've just been butchering and dressing a deer out back."

"Reason for the visit is that we barged into our cabin and interrupted a party this morning. A whole family of raccoons were feasting on our stores of foodstuff. Took all three of us to get them to skedaddle."

"Time of year the woodland critters are busy getting ready for winter snows. I have a contrivance that can be raised and lowered into position which I use when I'm away from the place. Rest of the time I make enough noise to show whose property this is. And of course I generally have a fire stoked at night."

"Well now that I've put some thought into it I feel confident that I will be able to design a setup that might can be left in place whether we're there or not. Helps a heap to see your apparatus. "

"I'll just bet you'll find success. Fact I'd put money on it, Jasper. When you've built the contraption I'd sure be interested in seeing it. What you fellows doing this day?"

"Same as you, Jake. Boys are out hunting and soon as they get back we'll be occupied with getting the meat ready for storing up."

"Always pleased to see you. One of these times we should plan a proper visit. Maybe share some whiskey and singsong."

"That sounds fine, Jake. I'll tell the boys so's to give them something to look forward to. Be seeing you."

Otis and Sam had dispatched a nice sized buck and had it strung up for dressing by the time I returned. I'd dragged a huge log down with me knowing that after it was chopped into pieces would be added to the rising stacks of firewood already under the tarp.

Us three worked steadily all afternoon and into the evening getting the game cut up into strips and folding each one over a rope tied to two trees. Then in the morrow planned to smoke it over the outside fire pit. We would have to hold vigil all night to keep animals away, but we could take it in shifts.

Before climbing onto my bough bed I spent some time at the creek scrubbing some of the dirt off my hands and face. Next time in Oro I will buy a bath. I need to get my clothes washed too. None of this had anything to do with Miss Poole. Did it?

The lovely Lucinda Poole. I shifted around on the lumpy, pokey mattress trying to get comfortable.

Occupations of Three Females

The first day of the school term was only a few days away. Isabelle felt that the preparations she and her friend had made would ensure that the opening would be quite special and fun. She had worked on a new beige gabardine skirt and because of its practical hue would see her through the year nicely.

The young women spent all their breakfast time talking about Lucinda's opening show. How outstanding the occasion would surely be.

Early evening found Lucinda dressing in her performance outfit and pinning her hair on top of her head for a more stylish look. She had pinched her cheeks and chewed down on her lips to bring color to her face.

"No matter. This is the best I can do." She told herself as she walked into the street with a measure of aplomb.

She entered Smithson's Hall just as the proprietor was lighting some oil lamps which would be placed strategically about the room. The effect was to lend a certain orange-like tinge to the atmosphere of the room.

He would not be opening the bar on nights when Lucinda performed. The audience needed to be a sober one. But to offset the price of whiskey he planned to charge a half dollar for admittance.

"Well, Lucinda, the big night is finally upon us. You don't appear to be overly nervous."

"No, Mr. Smithson, I'm quite calm. I feel happy to be performing at last. Do you think there will be much of an assembly?"

He doffed his bowler theatrically and spoke with enthusiasm, "I personally have been advertising this event up and down the Gulch for many days. Every person I encounter tells me that they will be in attendance come hell or high water. Um, beg pardon for my language, Miss."

And so, Lucinda used the next half hour practicing her tunes on the pianoforte. She was silently inclined to question the placement of the instrument against a side wall because her back would be to the audience. But it would do for tonight. There was no time now to make a change.

The hall filled up quickly as soon as Smithson opened wide the door. He was serving as her bodyguard as well as ticket seller and a Master of Ceremonies of sorts.

All who could find a place on one of several benches felt advantaged but also there were many men standing two deep along the walls. Lucinda stood when Smithson introduced her. She took a furtive glance around the hall seeing whiskers and beards but not faces. She admittedly was feeling quite self-conscious.

However, right near the front was her dear friend sitting next to Mrs. Tabor. Seeing these two smiling broadly caused her to relax her facial features. And then she breathed in deeply and sat on her stool.

Her first number was "Wayfaring Stranger" which she sang confidently as the words were familiar to her. She remembered her mother humming and singing the tune when she was but a young girl fussing with chickens in their farm yard.

She had a repertoire prepared and ran through the list as evening turned into night. Even with her back to her audience she sensed a quiet room with very few restless noises. Not even a cough nor whisper in the space.

After an hour and a half of singing she stood and turned to the people.

The space erupted with applause. She smiled and dipped her head towards them, but she didn't know to bow or curtsy. She'd never given thought to such a ritual. She was spared of any embarrassment regarding the matter because her audience clamored for one more song.

She ended the performance with "Oh, Shenandoah" which was laden with nostalgia for many of those present.

With that final song the evening's entertainment came to an end. Her dear friends had departed some minutes before the show ended; and Smithson was too busy to provide an escort for her to get home. And also the night sky was dark with cloud cover; the moon and stars would be of no help.

Lucinda stepped out into the street just as a man, me, appeared out of nowhere and spoke.

"May I be of assistance, Miss Poole?"

"I think not, my good man. I do not know you. Please leave me be!"

"Lucinda! I am right here. I turned back so that we may walk up the road together." Isabelle called out.

"Beg pardon, Ma'am. Not my intention to interlope."

Lucinda could not make out my features in the darkness. She dipped her head and walked away into the night with her friend.

"Who was that man? Did you know him?" Isabelle asked.

"Something about his manner and voice seemed familiar. But I can't quite place him."

"It wasn't your dentist, was it?"

"Dentist? Why I wouldn't know. I was in such distress that morning. It could have been a wild bear holding the tools and I would have willingly opened my mouth."

"Well, Lucinda. The smithy, Jasper Gratz, did you a superb service. Maybe you and I should walk up to the Printer Boy tomorrow so you can thank the man properly."

"What a good idea. I'm embarrassed that I didn't think of it myself. And I must pay him for his services." She wondered silently why that name resonated.

Over breakfast Otis and Sam and me were making plans to have a cabin celebration. None of us three knew much about how to arrange such an event.

"What say we walk over and ask Mrs. Tabor about a gathering? She seems to be the go-to authority regarding any number of particulars."

We agreed with Otis.

Leaving the Tabor store were two painted women from the shady side of town. One was highly rouged and gaily outfitted and the other was veiled for some reason, presumably to hide her identity. We men gave them a wide berth as we entered.

"I apologize, friends. Those gals generally do their shopping before I close at the end of the day so as not to mix with my regular customers. How may I serve you?"

"Howdy, Ma'am. I see a barrel of apples yonder. We'll take a dozen. Might be we will dry them so's to enjoy when the weather turns cold."

"Fine idea, Sam. Say, Mrs., how would fellows such as us go about setting up a shindig on the occasion of completing a cabin in the hills? We'd like to invite some Gulch folks to join in the merriment."

"Allow me to study on your idea for a moment, Mr. Gratz. For now though go right on ahead and look around the store, if you care to."

We looked at sacks of corn meal, sugar, coffee and salt; piles of muslin and canvas, small barrels of beans and rice, and two Sharps rifles displayed alongside a shovel and three hatchets. On the counter were a few candles and bricks of hard soap. That covered just about everything in the store.

After a short time the proprietress called us over to the counter.

"You need to consider a few things. First, invite your guests by way of a personal visit. Next, purchase the food and drink which will be offered. And then, decide if you will be presenting entertainment and make arrangements for this. And be sure to describe your trail directions to those you hope will attend."

The three of us exchanged prolonged stares before Otis spoke up.

"That is a tall order. It will surely take a full day, maybe two to get 'er done."

"If the occasion warrants the necessity to give it significance then there really are no shortcuts, I fear."

I said, "We will follow your good recommendations to the letter, Mrs. Tabor. One week from today we will have the party. Consider this your invitation, if you please. One of us will stop by with directions to the cabin. And many thanks to you."

"I might just close up the store in order to attend, gentlemen."

Right at that very moment there was a disturbance and loud yelling on the road. We moved into the street to see what was going on.

Three men from the Miner's Commission, which comprised law enforcement in the Gulch, were standing at the edge of an embankment opposite the storefront. They had a ruthless character cornered in some willows above the creek bed.

"Come out and be hung like a man!" Hollered a well set-up fellow in regular mining garb.

There followed some scuffling and shouts with plenty of cussing as the blackguard was dragged up onto the road and in quick order was hogtied with ropes. Shortly a veritable spectacle developed as men emerged out of shadows and buildings to bear witness to a trial and hanging.

Otis. Sam and me tried to peer around heads in order to catch a glimpse of the feckless individual. But the men who had captured him had quickly moved quite a way down the road. We could only guess at who was tied up.

"Let's just get on with our own business." I said.

So we found some creek boulders to sit on and then attempted a list of people to be invited, as well as a partial list of items to serve for refreshments.

"I'll go up to the Printer Boy and ask Cal Jackson and Judson. While I'm there I'll see about constructing a chimney cover at the forge."

"I'm of a mind to walk on down to the bottom and tell Tom Starr about it, and Sam, maybe can go along to Doc's. We can meet up again at the store here to see what to buy to eat and drink."

"If we think of others should we go ahead and issue an invite?"

"Course, Sam. But let's try to hold it at ten or so. If a rainstorm came along while all those people were up there we couldn't get half to fit inside the cabin for shelter. Let's meet up by Pepper's corral before the afternoon wastes away."

So off we went in different directions.

For my part I took a few hours to make a grate out of scraps. It turned out to be a handy piece of equipment.

As soon as I returned from the Printer Boy lugging my grate I went back into the store and purchased two large sacks of grain for Pepper. Winter would necessitate the need for grain as the ground would likely be snow covered and frozen.

And so it followed that Lucinda and me did not cross paths that day and would in all likelihood not meet again for many days or even weeks to come.

Up at the cabin the day of the party began with a soft rain shower. This concerned us as we emerged one by one from the warm lodge. But then by mid-morning the sky cleared and a bright sun bathed the hillside. Rain droplets dried on the leaves and tree branches and the day promised to be warm and fine.

I walked into the back corral to have a word with Pepper.

"Okay you four legged bundle of vexation, I'm only going to tell you this one time so pay close attention. Some good folks from over the Gulch are visiting this afternoon. If you can find it in your heart to be the cause of no disturbance of any kind, I mean no little critter to startle, no loud noise to make you skittish. If you do anything to cause me aggravation, I will drag you back to Oro and sell you for a pinch of dust."

Pepper showed little interest in my speech. He pawed the needles in the dark earth and jerked and shook his head.

Jake Morgan was the first guest to appear in the yard and was given a hearty welcome by his friends. Sam was finishing a fire ring which would be put to use in several ways presently. Otis and me were rolling large logs into the yard for seating. Next Sam set up a good sized spit and began piercing a large roast of deer and threading it onto a stout pointed stick. That done, a huge fire was set ablaze and Otis went down to the nearby stream to fill a large pot so that the rabbits could be stewed.

"Now we have a half barrel of beer for drink and coffee as well. And I think that will be our offerings for this party. Am I missing anything, boys?"

"Not for our part, Jasper. But I'm sure looking forward to Doc's offering of biscuits. And Mrs. Tabor said she'd be bringing something special. Let's have us a cup of coffee and sit and relax for a spell. This party business is demanding work." Said Otis.

Otis went into the cabin to retrieve the pot of coffee off the inside stove. He also carried out a bag of salt and sprinkled the meat and stew generously.

"Did you remember to bring along a cup, Jake?"

"Sure did. I brought two extras in case they might be needed. Lem'me get those cups and some tin plates from my saddle bag before I sit and enjoy my coffee."

"Mighty useful supplies, Jake. And we surely do thank you," I said. "Without your help we'd be in a pickle, wouldn't we, boys?"

During a compatible half hour before voices and horses were heard approaching on the hillside, I showed my chimney grate to an impressed Jake. I then hastened to Pepper's small stable.

"Now we've a group of friendly people to welcome. None of your stunts, you hear? And you're sharing this space. So be seemly."

I came back around the cabin just as folks were dismounting.

"Howdy and welcome to all! Come around back here and tie off your animals to Pepper's hitching rail. My burro is good as gold and doesn't mind a bit." At this Pepper shifted his feet and swished his tail.

"Where's Mrs. Tabor? She hiking up later?"

"Hi ya, Otis. Says she has to stay at the store and wait for the freight to come by as she's expecting a large order from down by Alma." Said Doc and he added, "She sent two large cans of peaches, said it was her contribution."

"Aw. She ought to hire a worker to help out. The woman never gets a day off. Too bad ol' HAW spends month after month prospecting over at Buckskin Joe. Leaves it to the Mrs. to keep them from going belly-up." Said Doc.

One at a time the visitors poked their heads into the open doorway to see how the cabin's interior stacked up. All were very positive in their individual assessments. Then they shuffled into the yard and settled themselves onto one log or another. Besides Doc the men included Judson, Cal, Tom Starr, and two fellows Sam and Otis worked the placers with - Charlie and Joe. It was a congenial gathering.

Otis kept busy watching over the rabbit stew and the spitted venison. He also placed a large skillet of biscuits, complements of Doc, off to one side of the fire ring.

Savory smells from the yard were wafting out into the nearby woods. Chances of attracting critters were considerable. Although for now all over the woods everything seemed to be basking in a gentle quietude.

Judson took a mouth organ from his shirt pocket and began to softly play a familiar melody. Snatches of easy conversations sprang up around the yard.

After an hour or so Otis and Sam rolled the beer barrel into the yard. This caused a stirring amongst the group. No one had expected such an offering. Each one to a man spilled out the coffee and readied his cup for drinking from the beer barrel.

Such good natured ribbing and joking helped the group to bond and added a familial feel to that high mountain meadow.

In good time the guests were served slices of roast venison and plates of rabbit stew. Doc's skillet of flaky biscuits was passed around the circle. All washed down with a seemingly endless supply of beer.

Once the food had been consumed and all were satiated, quite without warning the mules and horses sounded out a cacophony of stressed screams.

"Oh no! Now what has come over Pepper? He's been a pip all afternoon, but now what?" I asked, automatically blaming the burro as I leaped to my feet and flew to the corral.

The scene before us was one of petrified animals all bucking to get free of the rail. Every man was attempting to calm his animal when Jake shushed us and pointed to an uphill stand of aspen.

"It's a mountain lion skulking around the area. Grab your guns and make some noise. He'll likely run off." Jake told us.

This action did the trick as far as we could tell. But no one had aimed to wound or kill the wild cat so he might likely show up again on some future day. The last we saw of the smallish cat was a patch of caramel colored fur streaking up the mountainside.

It took a goodly amount of time to calm the animals and after they settled each was offered a fistful of grain as an appeasement.

For once Pepper didn't appear to have been the ring leader which amazed me and I said as much aloud.

"Whoa ho, Pepper. Don't get a swelled head but I'm the first to say 'sorry' when I've falsely accused you of wrong doing. Although, you do have a reputation for being an instigator. And three or four fellows will back me up on this point."

Pepper ran through a number of favored behaviors - stomping, pawing the ground, snorting, and much tossing of his head.

"Okay, I get your message. Doesn't mean every past infraction is forgotten, though. Just remember."

Back in the yard the men were making signals to indicate that the party had played itself out and it was time to make their way back to the Gulch. Handshakes and complements all around and the gang was away.

Jake remained with his buddies to help with cleanup. We set him up with a chunk of deer meat, but had no way for the stew to be transported. The biscuits were gone but …

"Hey ya, Jake, you might make yourself a pallet in the cabin and then tomorrow we could just continue the eating and drinking of all the party offerings. What say you to that, now?"

"I can't think of any tasks at my place that would have me rushing back to see about. I'd enjoy your company for an additional number of hours. You bet. Thanks to you, Jasper, Otis, Sam."

After storing the food so that critters couldn't get to it we settled in for the night.

Lucinda Tumbles Again

During the time that the party was in progress Lucinda and Isabelle took a walk up to the Printer Boy to seek out the dentist. They found no one about the property, however. So they retraced their steps back down the way they'd come.

"Oh Isabelle, isn't this just so disappointing? Once determined to do something worthwhile one hopes that providence would intercede. I am most utterly disheartened about this venture."

"No need to be so crestfallen. It is but a momentary cloud crossing the sun."

Oro looked peaceful, the creeks lazy and sun dazzled. The drone of insects followed the two women as they entered the hall.

The smells in the room mingled together - food and unwashed people. They sat down to a lunch of beans and cornbread. Food was rarely a cause for enjoyment. It was merely consumed to sustain life in this mining camp and many others just like it.

After lunch Lucinda spent the remainder of the afternoon looking down at the street through the dust and fly specked window of her room. Her mood was melancholy.

And then her thoughts began to swarm round and round. She began pacing back and forth in the room, wringing her hands. She felt she was again on the wagon train. She could see her new husband walking away from her into the nearby trees. Her breathing was quickening and her heart pounding. She was waiting for her dear Tobias. Oh why isn't he back yet? And then the horrible news. She wanted to forget the pain, the anguish and distress of standing by helplessly as the snake's poison consumed the man she loved. Her mind spiraled back to the lonely months which followed. Tears were now spilling from her eyes. She couldn't seem to bring herself back into the present.

To the now of Oro City.

She pushed back against a desire to float into the velvety influence of laudanum. While more than once she had noted the cobalt bottles of this substance in Tabor's store, why on a day such as this would her mind become awash with a feverish need to caress oblivion?

But after some little time she realized that she would indeed succumb to temptation. And so she hurried into the store across the road and made a purchase. Once back in her chamber she uncapped the bottle and tipped the substance down her throat.

The next day and the one following Isabelle climbed the stairs to her friend's room and rapped on the door. There was no answer. Frank White was reluctant to use his key to gain entrance. But on the third day Isabelle's doggedness paid off and she was allowed entry into her friend's room.

What greeted her was quite disturbing to see, for Lucinda was sprawled on the bed fully clothed and indeed yet wearing her button shoes. Her hair was in complete disarray, knotted and tangled. Her face was devoid of color, grey tinged. Also the flesh around her closed eyes was smudged a purplish hue.

"Lucinda, my dear, what is this all about? Please lift your head so that I may see into your eyes."

Getting no response, Isabelle wrapped her arms around her friend and coaxed her to try to sit up. Then she loosened Lucinda's bodice ties and removed two petticoat layers. Next she undid the shoes and leaned over to place the pair beside the bed. Doing this last part she spied the nearly empty tell-tale blue bottle poking out from under the bed.

She emitted a gasp and choked down a sob.

"Oh, woe is me, my dearest friend! I am sorely distraught to see you thus."

Isabelle paced the floor trying to devise some kind of strategy. She had knowledge of the consequences of laudanum because her mother's sister who had the misfortune of a breech during childbirth needed much help to alleviate the pain of the ordeal. The effect of the medicine was that her aunt would be plagued by an addiction to laudanum that followed her into an early grave.

Spontaneously the school teacher decided to push opening day one week later. She left hurriedly and once the notice was posted on the school door entrance she returned to Lucinda's bedside. The only way she could think to nurse her friend was to apply cold wet cloths to her forehead. Lucinda was beginning to open her eyes at intervals and struggling to climb off the bed.

"Lucinda, please don't attempt to get up. You are yet incapacitated from the laudanum and must allow me to nurse you back to health."

"Oh no. All I need is some more of my elixir." Her eyes darted about the room and stopped when she saw the blue bottle on her small table.

Isabelle chided herself mentally for not disposing of the bottle immediately.

"Here, here, then. I will hand it over."

There was no more than a few drops left and Isabelle surmised that this wouldn't tip the scale one way or another. Lucinda put the bottle to her lips and licked down the drops. She ran her tongue into the opening and sighed.

"I'm feeling a little better. But I will absolutely need another refill presently." She grasped her friend's hand and implored her to cross the road to fetch a fresh supply.

Isabelle was in anguish and knew not where to turn for counsel. She only knew that her dear Lucinda needed constant vigilance if there was to be even a slight chance for recovery. So she entered Tabor's store and approached the counter.

"May I be of assistance, Miss Isabelle?" Augusta Tabor sensed that the school teacher was suffering some distress.

"Oh, my mind is in turmoil as I feel such an obligation to map a course out of this quandary. You see, Madam, I am vexed about the future health of our Lucinda. A few days ago she consumed a full bottle of laudanum and today when the landlord and I finally gained entrance to her room we found her lying on her bed unconscious and yet fully clothed. At first I assumed that she had merely succumbed to the vapors." She took some deep breaths before continuing.

"On further examination I noticed a blue bottle on the floor near the bed. Passing the opening under my nose apprised me of the contents."

"Where is Lucinda presently?"

"She sent me here on a fool's errand to fetch another cobalt colored bottle."

"I am going to make an extremely radical recommendation, my dear. One that I feel you will regard with a great deal of repugnance and consternation."

"It is of no consequence. Please just advise me." And then I was guided to a bench on the far wall and bade to sit.

"Isabelle, you are doubtless aware of the ladies of easy virtue who live down yonder on 'the row'. You will be scandalized by my proposal, however I think it may be Lucinda's slim chance for a recovery."

Isabelle's face turned red and her breathing was suddenly rapid and then she was assaulted with a case of hiccups. She feared she might faint but Mrs. Tabor rushed to give her a cup of water. From the cup she flicked several drops onto the younger woman's flushed face.

When at last she was able to draw a deep breath Isabelle exclaimed, "Why no decent woman would venture over to the shady side of town to converse with such brazen creatures!"

"Of course I know that this is true, but I'm not suggesting that you are the person to make such an assignation. You see it is because of my role as storekeeper that I know of the possibility of such a prospect."

And then quite succinctly this wise woman described how and why and when all this could come about.

Isabelle was feeling less lightheaded and scandalized when she scurried back to her friend's bedside.

"Mrs. Tabor and I have a strategy in place with the intent of getting you through this present malady. For now though I have instructions on what will be a manageable dosage of the blue bottle syrup. You may not like the way all this must be done. But here it is. I will give you a spoonful twice daily and keep the bottle in my possession."

"No. No. This plan will not do. I simply won't have it." Lucinda was seated at the table where the window faces the street. She then crossed the room and stood close to her friend. "I must have the medicine right here with me in case I need it during the night. I have terrible dreams that keep me awake."

Isabelle had much to think about and could no longer stay. She left the room while pocketing the laudanum.

Inevitably, Lucinda was left alone to churn and stew in her poor addled mind.

The Brink of Ruination

Millie Osmond was 14 years old when she left her family's Missouri farm to join the wagons going west. Just before leaving home her parents, considering their seven younger children, married her off to a no-account rover. Millie knew very little about the world and just about nothing of the lands they would be traveling. Truly, she was as strong in body and spirit as her new husband, Will Abbot, was weak.

Most of Millie's story is a series of mishaps and tragedies.

She found herself with child only four months after beginning the journey. The couple owned three sorry looking cows to offer for trade. And with these they had been able to procure a wagon, one which looked as if it wouldn't last ten miles, never mind a westward trip of many hundreds of miles.

Millie's baby was born in the Kansas Territory where she and Will had been living in their wrecked wagon for a month. Because of an extensively bent rear axle both back wheels had fallen to the wayside.

Will had made a wretched name for himself while with the train and no man was sympathetic nor willing to offer aid. He had proven himself to be a confounded fool who would take no advice. After some days the stranded family had no food nor any other useful supplies, so the man decided to trek back four miles to an Indian village to get help.

Will lacked the wherewithal to properly convey his requests

to the Natives. He was rude and had such an air of entitlement that they had no compunction at all for ending his sorry life right there and then.

Millie had waited nearly a week for his return when another train sighted her ruined wagon and rescued her and the babe. She told the wagon master about her missing husband and how he'd left days before to look for help among the Indian villagers.

The wagon master held out no hope that Will was still alive and convinced Millie to travel with his train. He found another widow driving her own wagon who would welcome help and female companionship, and doubtless the very young mother was grateful.

Millie was quite honestly relieved to be free of Will and felt wholly able to manage her life and that of her baby girl on her own.

And then even more tragedy struck.

Many on the train were enduring severe bouts of dysentery. It wasn't long before Millie and her baby were stricken by this dread wretchedness. The baby only lasted two days before death claimed her.

They buried the infant six feet from the wagon ruts. Millie felt the painful loss deep within her heart but even more so because the burial place was so desolate. She lamented that she would never again be able to find the grave. Not ever.

Emotional instability threatened her well-being now and again, but one way or another she always managed to drag herself away from languishing in sorrow.

Eventually Millie came to the confluence of the South Platte River and Cherry Creek and a young Denver City at the base of the formidable mountain ranges.

Millie was not one to succumb to the ordeals of life's events. Indeed she had an adventurous outlook and was intrigued by accounts of prospectors finding vast riches. She found employment behind the counter of a mercantile and saved all her wages. Within a couple of months she had enough to buy a ticket on a stagecoach heading to the gold fields deep in the mountains.

And so it was that 16 year old Millie Abbot came to Oro City.

It didn't take much imagination to realize how or why the young woman ended up on the shady side of Oro. She hadn't any choices, and she needed a livelihood. She absolutely had no interest in being married again. Life on the row afforded her the only option. Shelter, food, and income.

Millie climbed out of the stagecoach when it stopped a few miles up the Gulch road. It was mid-summer but the air was cool and thin. The placers afforded the dankness of raw earth scooped from creek beds. She was perplexed and stood still staring around at her surroundings.

Inhaling deeply she stopped at the entrance to a boarding house. The contrast of daylight and indoor dimness made focusing strenuous. Several minutes seemed to pass before she spotted an odd looking fellow, short of stature, bespectacled, and dressed in miner's garb.

He approached. But then he stood there saying nothing so

Millie was forced to address him.

"Sir, I am needful for a place to reside. I find myself completely at loose ends in this district. Would you be so kind as to advise me?"

Speaking with a pronounced Scottish accent he said, "Women do not stay here in my business place. Only miners."

"Where would a female find shelter?"

"Go up to Tabor's store past three bends in the road. Ask in there."

And so she walked uphill along a dusty, rutted road, passing around one bend and around another and finally a third. She could see the store front from a ways off.

Once inside she approached a counter behind which a rather plain, dark haired woman stood ciphering a list of items.

"Madam, I am newly arrived in this place and have been told that I might find lodging within. I am quite respectable and also anticipative. My name is Millie Abbot, a widow from Missouri."

"I am Augusta Tabor, sometime proprietress of this emporium and most often awaiting the return of my prospecting husband. He spends an inordinate number of months over Mosquito Pass in Buckskin Joe. He will likely come along with the first snows.

"In answer to your query, there are two rooms in the upstairs attic. I share one with my absent husband and the other is used by Maxcy, our son. But Maxcy is presently up at Buckskin Joe with the Mister until his schooling takes back up. So, I am happy to have you use the room. I charge a modest dollar per night."

Millie signed a ledger and was shown the room. Once alone she sat on the bed which had an ordinary corn husk mattress covered with two very thin blankets.

"This will be suitable for my simple needs. I must count my money and make certain that I can pay for this lodging." She spoke to no one but herself.

An audible inhale. "Three dollars of folding money and some coins!"

First splashing water from the provided bowl she peered into a small mirror left behind by a previous boarder. Her wavy auburn hair was her singular vanity, and now she attempted to smooth errant hair strands before donning her bonnet. She owned so little that one small shelf held everything.

Once more out on the road she ambled back down from whence the stage had left her off. Music was drifting out from a saloon. Instinctively she was hesitant to enter, but knowing not why precisely that she shouldn't. Life on the wagon train afforded some clues, but nothing of practical matters, and absolutely nothing about this type of establishment.

Furthermore, Millie's upbringing gave her hints about pretty much nothing except farm life. And now that she was out in the wide world all was cloaked in mystery. Quite suddenly a woman approached her from within the hall.

"You look lost and unsettled in this lowly mining town. I'm guessing that you are freshly arrived and yet green from the farm?"

Before offering a response Millie took some time to study this person, chancing a display of crude manners. Surprisingly the woman was not bonneted which placed her carefully coiffed black hair on display. The yellow and brown gown she was wearing had too many ruffles to count. Flounces of filmy fabric covered her arms and she was holding a parasol which seemed frivolous in this dusty colorless and foul-smelling place.

"You are correct. I have just arrived on a stagecoach from Auraria. Have you lived here very long?"

"About a year or so. When I first set foot in Oro City it was mid- springtime, but even so it snowed for ten days in a row. It may as well have been mid-winter. I had to wrap up in a blanket with my cloak underneath.

"By the by, my name's Hazel. Anyhow at the first I took up with four gals who'd been living in a large tent that was crowded and uncomfortable. It did have a stove which kept out a bit of the snow and freezing drafts. One night I stumbled against that very stove and burned my arm bad. You see the scar?" Hazel went on, "Well, dearie, before a month was gone the miners built this here saloon with rooms above and the five of us just up and settled into comfort."

"Oh, my!" Millie thought to herself. "Ladies of easy virtue!"

And to Hazel, "I must away. I have someone who awaits me at the Mercantile." She turned and hurried back up the road.

The next time we see Millie she surprises us by having swallowed her pride along with the damping down of her convictions. Eventually she joins the fallen angels in this house of ill fame and her destiny threatens to take an abrupt downward swing.

This particular brothel above a saloon was operated by a Madam Red Stockings from St. Joe. She was a shrewd woman who after having established a bordello in Oro City knew it was good business to make certain that each of her girls followed a set of guidelines. In part the directives included hygiene, a type of dress code, and how much dust a client could expect to pay for a variety of services.

Miners would pay on a percentage basis: 25-50 cents for a dance, 50 cents for liquor, 25 cents for a bath and so forth. These prices were in addition to actual time spent in a room with a girl, $2. And so, for these set prices a client could expect protection from nasty behaviors such as cheating a man out of his money in any manner of ways. The Madam took a cut off the top of each of her gal's interactions to pay expenses.

Expenditures for comfort were many for a high-end sporting house, in contrast to what chippies on the line spent. Bathing was paramount, sicknesses were taken care of, and rooms had serviceable beds, although disease was unavoidable.

Moreover, Red Stockings took pains to keep her girls' spirits buoyed up with birthday celebrations and parties. She needed no cat-fighting nor suicides in her establishment. Whores were a very valuable commodity in a mining camp.

And so, it wasn't very long before Millie's last nickel was spent. She faced a future that would send her soul to perdition, or not, depending on whether fate would intervene in time to change her social standing.

Late one summer morning she entered the saloon and asked the bartender where she might find a Madam Red Stockings. He pointed to the stairs and said the room on the right at the top was where this woman would be found.

Millie climbed the stairs and then rapped lightly on the door but was made to wait some long minutes before a reply came.

"Must I remind whoever is out there that business hours begin at seven o'clock?"

"Yes. I mean my name is Millie Abbot of late from Missouri." She felt intimidated talking through a closed door, but continued, "I am hopeful for a position here."

Presently the door opened and a woman ushered her in. Red Stockings had hair piled in elaborate layers, and she was swathed in a fussy garment meant as a dressing gown. She crossed to a small table and sat down in a rather ornate chair, and then motioned for Millie to sit upon a fainting couch across the room.

"You are very young. Tell me why you are here."

Millie felt frumpy in her worn drab dress and droopy bonnet. To save time she began in the middle rather than the beginning of her story. "Well you see I lost my babe to the dysentery on the wagon trail and before that my husband got kilt by Indians. Then I came up here on a stage using up the last of my money. I don't like the notion of starving and freezing. And that is why I am here."

The madam took a few minutes to ruminate before responding, so Millie made use of the lapse to look about the room. A lacy curtain covered the window, and there was an elaborate lamp with a red glass ball placed upon a table that stood along one wall. The coverlets on the bed and the fainting couch were heavy brocades. Everything in the room was sumptuous and colorful.

The madam was wearing red stockings and had a second pair on her small side table needing repairs and so just now she picked one up and also a needle before speaking again.

"Before I ask you to stay it's important that you know what goes on in this place. Do you?"

"Um, yes I think so. I believe the intent is to give comfort to the miners so that they'll feel less lonesome."

"Millie, is it? You must know that in this establishment time is money. The idea is to spend as little time as is necessary with each customer, so no lingering, and then afterwards simply usher him out with no fuss. Matter of policy is that the clients pay up front with dust. No money is given to my whores. I pay them at the end of each week. Understand?"

Sighing deeply Millie nodded. She thought that the interview had not been successful. She felt such a lack of experience and worldliness.

As she rose to take her leave Madam requested that she return in the morrow to be measured for a gown.

"Oh! How wonderful." She said to herself.

Alas! She was so naïve and innocent.

Life as a demi monde in a bordello had its routines like any other profession would. And in a house full of women dramas of one kind or another constantly cropped up. But for Millie, after a prolonged time of coming to terms with being a whore, she had yet to be handed an assignation. The other harlots in the house were unwilling to hand over clients to one with no proficiencies nor experiences.

It was during this time that Lucinda had continued to strain against the abhorrent restrictions placed upon her by Isabelle. She remained angry throughout the days and nights due to a withdrawal from the laudanum. In fact, the very sight of Isabelle coming through her door made her rant and rave, the reason being that her friend had no business meddling in her affairs.

Her room was in a constant state of disarray. Food had been thrown against walls. The few clothes she owned had been reduced to shreds during fits of fury. The flimsy mattress was of no use as the insides were now covering the floor, which made the place look like a barnyard. The smell was so repugnant that in order to take a breath one must cover their nose.

As for Isabelle, no friend could have endured such atrocities and insults and with more kindness and patience as she herself had been doing for days. However, she was beginning to lose heart. She had been suffering in various ways right along with her friend. Her heart was filled with such anguish and frustration that she doubted she could go on for much longer.

After six days of maltreatment a miracle materialized from a most unlikely source. Augusta Tabor intervened and implored Madam Red Stockings to supply one of her soiled doves as a nurse for Lucinda.

The Madam said that she could not spare any of her regulars but she had a new recruit who would likely be willing to take on such an assignment.

A not quite fallen angel in the person of Millie Abbot turned up on the seventh morning to be greeted by Isabelle on the stoop of the boarding house.

The very young woman was a wonder in many ways. She did not look the part of one of her profession because of several factors: to wit, a modest gown of subtle fashion, a hairdo plainly designed, and a face free of excessive rouge and lip color. Madam had orchestrated the girl's appearance by way of Mrs. Tabor's urgings.

Isabelle had been forewarned of the source whereof her rescuer heralded. She did refrain from making judgements and instead embraced this unlikely supplier of nursing help.

"Millie, I for one am grateful for your presence in these parts. My dear friend, Lucinda, is in need of a nurse. We, that is myself and Mrs. Tabor, would like to offer you employment for an unknown number of weeks."

"I don't know very much about the skills required of a nurse," Millie said.

"Please consider following me to the hillside yonder. Our interview is best conducted out of view of curious onlookers."

And so once seated on some sizable rocks Isabelle told the tale.

It was agreed that from the outset Millie would stay with Lucinda round the clock. Augusta had a second mattress sent up to the room. When seeing this change in her living space Lucinda fell into a state of deep despair. She knew that a conspiracy was afoot to keep her from descending deeply and often into the laudanum bottle. She despised her friend Isabelle for her traitorous ways. And she abhorred the young nurse as an interloper. However, Millie proved herself to be resilient and reliable.

On the bad days there were tantrums and on the good days sulking and imploring. The latter to the point of groveling. Millie was impervious to all of Lucinda's behaviors. She was intent on helping her charge overcome the torments of addiction with every ounce of energy which she possessed.

The drug indeed complicated therapy by its being readily available in the mercantile. One morning before dawn a scheming Lucinda fled her dwelling and hid behind an abandoned placer claim on the creek. Her frenzied idea was to entreat some hapless miner to make a purchase on her behalf.

Millie, however, awoke and sounded the alarm before Lucinda's plan could be put into play. Four persons, that is the landlord, the nurse, the store mistress, and the friend, searched the immediate vicinity and found the runaway just as the sun was rising over the ridgeline.

After that day Landlord Frank White installed a second lock of sorts. Millie was in possession of the singular key which made her daily routine a bit less stressful. She left the room only to buy food which was supplied through Isabelle and Augusta at the mercantile. And additionally, Augusta paid wages to Millie during this time when she was nursing Lucinda.

During these many weeks my pards and me had been putting

up stores which would see us through the long winter months. Sam and Otis both had become sharpshooters when it came to hunting game. The cave on the hillside was well stocked with meat.

Us three men, and sometimes Jake, were constantly refining the woodsy dwelling. For instance, we laid flat sided logs in front of the doorway so that snow could be stomped from our boots and kept outdoors rather than being tracked indoors. And we added more shelves on the inside walls for the purpose of storage. We figured that the floor should be kept uncluttered for ease of moving about.

And to guarantee comfort for Pepper during snowy days we built a roof over his corral and nailed some boards along the exposed portion which might also keep his water from freezing in the pail, although this last part was a far-flung notion. And finally straw and dried grasses were strewn generously on the ground. Pepper was indeed given considerations that the average beast never would have been.

"You boys have devised a fresh idea with the stoop." Said Jake one soft sunny fall day. "I am going to add one to the front of my cabin within the week. Well, I'm off to finish up some chores that need attention."

"You've been good and generous since we first journeyed into these parts, Jake. We consider you a prized friend. A brick among fellows." I spoke for the others as I did more often than not.

And later, "What say we hike into the Gulch for a look around? It's been nigh on three weeks and if nothing else we could use the trip to refill our whiskey jugs." Said Otis.

Sam sat whittling by the fire ring and nodded his assent. As for myself constant thoughts of Lucinda for several days filled my mind. I'd been hoping for a chance meeting. Now I said, "I am agreeable to this plan. We might even put in a day or two of work before the winter snows catch us."

Since the morning was not yet half spent we tidied up around the cabin and secured the chimney grate. Then after tying a lead onto Pepper, we immediately set out on what had become a well-worn trail through the woods.

Pepper brought up the rear and as usual seemed to relish nudging my hind end while climbing any of the three inclines.

"Stop that confounded pushiness, you scoundrel! You'd be cautioned to stay on my good side if you fancy any apples in the future."

Once again the road along the Gulch was teeming with activity. At least six new cabins graced the hillsides of upper Oro since us men had last been there. Several freights could be spotted with teams of mules pulling heavy loads. Goods for building structures, mining equipment implements, and various food supplies were piled high on the wagons.

Aside from all this, dogs were a recent addition to the settlement. Two mangy curs were just now barking at the legs of a mule. The skinner was not pleased and attempted to quirt them as he passed. The dogs were too cagey to be hit though, and ran off in the direction of the garbage dumps which would doubtless afford them ample scraps to feed on.

The air was thick with dust and smells of horse droppings and of course, flies everywhere. The mid-autumn sun felt uncomfortable because of the layers of clothing the three of us always wore. Earlier we had agreed to pay Mrs. Tabor a visit so as to hear what the scuttlebutt was for the day.

Entering the store I said, "Say Mrs. T., what's been doing in the Gulch since we've been up in the woods at our cabin? Anything of interest will satisfy our privation, as our brains are so stuffed with the prattle of each other's chitchat that we may already have nothing but dust in our heads."

"It's always a sunnier day when you come into my mercantile, Gents. It seems that news of any kind is much the same from week to week. Let's see now, a misfortunate incident happened two days ago when a man filled with whisky fell from his saddle and toppled beneath the horse's hooves. He left this world with a crushed skull."

Otis asked, "Was he someone known hereabouts?"

"No. He had only just newly arrived."

We each nodded and were turning to leave when the Mrs. spoke again. "A sad situation which I don't relish speaking about concerns a young woman known to you, Jasper. I relate the story because I feel you can be trusted to keep mum. In fact before continuing I must have your promise, each of you, to keep what I say close to the vest."

"We do agree, don't we, boys?" Otis and Sam nod yes.

And so Mrs. T told the tale of strife and wretchedness

surrounding the dulcet Lucinda. She left out the part about Millie, the almost prostitute, having been asked to nurse the young woman.

"If you want regular updates on Lucinda's convalescence I suggest you ask the schoolmarm, Isabelle, as she is a close confidant of Lucinda's."

Downcast and dismayed with hands in my pockets I left the store with my friends and stood speechless on the road for several minutes. I could not reconcile the memory of purity and sweetness with this story of depravity.

"You men go along to Doc's and I'll be along in due time. I need to take some minutes alone."

Sam and Otis nodded solemnly and headed down the road toward Doc's.

Several minutes later I ambled over to Pepper's corral. I often took comfort in being near the burro, petting his coarse fur and speaking my thoughts aloud. It seemed an odd sort of therapy but not uncommon in these times.

"I just don't know what to think. She was always so proper and the very picture of respectability. No one could fault her sense of decorum, now could they, Pepper? I just don't know how to feel or what to think." I repeated.

Just then sounds of children laughing and shouting reached my ears.

"School must be let out for the day." And patting Pepper's snout once more I turned towards the school.

Kids were scampering along the road; the game was "Tag,

you're it!" and one little girl tripped and fell, skinning her knee. Two older boys began tussling when one called the other a sissy. I counted six students.

Isabelle stood in the school door and beckoned for the pair of older boys to run back to her.

"You may both go inside and clean the schoolroom from top to bottom. When you have completed the task report back to me."

I approached Isabelle not sure how to begin a discourse. The teacher resolved my hesitancy when she spoke.

"Sir, I remember you from a time several weeks ago. You had just extracted my friend's rotten tooth and were helping her to walk down this very road."

"Madam, my name is Jasper Gratz. I've been in the hills working on a cabin with my friends, so I have just now heard the distressing story about Lucinda Poole. Mrs. Tabor related the events with immense discretion and sympathy.

"I was hoping for some additional details that might explain why and how this fair young woman has ended up in the midst of such a heinous state of circumstances."

"My good man, I do not know you nor do I see any valid reason that would lead me to share information with you about my friend."

A horse and rider galloped by as we stood talking. The man was rough looking and callous to be riding at such speeds in the Gulch. Here about was an understanding that such recklessness was against the governing laws of Oro City. The rider turned his horse around at the Printer Boy Mine and was again passing the spot where Isabelle and me were standing.

I stepped near to the horseman's path and beckoned him to slow the horse. This was an impetuous action that could have gone either way.

"Friend, it is a common practice to slow your horse to a walk here in the Gulch. Folks might think you're running from the law. And furthermore, school's just left off for the day. Children walking all along the road." I said.

"Okay, fella. I'll gentle my horse along until I get where I'm going. First saloon I see." And then he slowly trotted off.

This bit of drama made a positive impression on Isabelle by revealing a particle of my so-called decent character. She brushed at her skirt in a fruitless attempt to be rid of some dustiness before speaking.

"I could disclose to you stories and stories. But it is my belief that it is a person's due right to tell their own story, Sir. My dear friend, Lucinda, may not like me divulging particulars in regards to her past or present life."

"I appreciate your sense of loyalty. I guess I was hoping to learn of Lucinda's recovery, or rather when such a time might be predicted that she would once again be singing at Smithson's. You see, I have a longing in my heart to know her once again as she was on the wagon train coming west."

"I cannot see into the future, but I do feel safe in telling you that gradual progress is becoming apparent with each passing day."

"We haven't been properly introduced. Would it be polite to ask you your name?"

"Isabelle Laughlin. And now I will offer a plan of sorts for future mutual exchanges. If you would be agreeable to such."

"I would like to hear your offer."

"It is quite simple really. On days when you're in Oro City you might stop by the schoolhouse at the beginning or end of the day, but not while my classes are in session. If on those days I have updates of Lucinda to share, you will find yourself the recipient of my reports. Does this seem to be an acceptable way forward, Mr. Gratz?"

Me and the schoolmarm each went our separate ways pleased with our newfound allegiance.

Now I walked down the road towards Doc's, but as I drew near to Lucinda's Holiday House I slowed my pace and looked up at her window. At least I guessed it was hers because of a fluttering curtain.

As I stood there I removed my hat and slapped it against my leg. The young woman's sufferings made me so unhappy. I wasn't a prayerful man but I would love to have Father Dyer come along and intone one of his readings from The Good Book on Lucinda's behalf.

Before walking away I wiped the sweat from my brow and replaced the worn black hat. I had not been told about Millie Abbot's part in all this but felt sure that some person might be nursing Lucinda. One final look at the window revealed that someone's hand was moving the curtain aside. Who's hand?

Not one thing could I do for her that I could think of. I felt that I would keep trying to figure out a way to be of help, but I really didn't hold out for much hope.

Dejectedly plodding along towards Doc's I noticed that Oro City was filled with the noise of the building. Hammering and sawing of boards. Plenty of voices raised to be heard above the general clamor. And more and more people out and about. The town seemed to be growing faster than anyone might have foreseen.

"What's the word, Doc? I can't figure out the crowds of people and all the new building going on. I was of the belief that the gold was most nearly played out."

"Howdy, Jasper. There's work digging a ditch that will bring water from the Evans Gulch right into the placers. Be awhile 'fore it's dug. That gulch is some miles away to the north of here. Heard talk that something called hydraulic power would wash away entire hills so's the gold that's still around can be mined. Don't understand the exact nature of the methods, but some men are sure gung ho about it."

"Whew! That's going to mean big changes all around here, I'm guessing."

"The Printer Boy's still bringing them in here. But even so that ditch won't be finished for a good year or more. Winter's coming on before you know it. But for now the quartz gold sure keeps folks fired up and they'll keep a 'coming. And building.

Your buddies said they were going for a whiskey. Got tired of waiting on you, huh?"

"Sounds about right, Doc. Guess I'll go along to the saloon. After a while we'll be back for the night."

I walked into Smithson's but it was tomb-like. So I looked across the road and saw that one recently erected building was teeming with miners. I strolled across to the swinging doors of the entrance.

Getting into this place was a bit tricky and took some jostling and shoving. Rough men don't generally take to being pushed around and mostly will become belligerent at the drop of a hat. So it was timely that Otis appeared and led me to a space at the bar where he and Sam were standing.

"Hi ho, Jasper. We was thinking that you must of taken a wrong turn and ended up over in Iowa Gulch. Lost." Said Sam.

"Nope. That sounds more like you than me. See. I'm too smart to go faltering about in the wrong direction. In case either of you care to listen I just found out why all this building activity is a ramping up. A reason aside from mining at the Printer Boy."

Otis ordered a fresh round of whiskeys and said, "Sure we're interested. Ain't we, Sam?"

"Doc was telling about a ditch being dug from the distant Evans Gulch over to this here gulch. To go along with the ditch there's a hint of something called hydraulic power arriving in the not too distant future to be used for getting at the gold still buried in the hillsides. And that's what the additional creek water is needed for."

Otis and Sam exchanged skeptical looks.

Slowly shaking his head Otis said, "Have you been sipping on whisky before meeting us here?"

"Think you know better than that."

"Well, making up a tall tale and expecting us to swallow it down whole is not very neighborly, Jasper."

"I just got through saying that it was Doc told me about this ditch. I didn't dream it up just to get your goat."

We trailed back up to Doc's but supper was no longer being served. Looking around the place we spotted Doc walking from the kitchen and went over to him.

"Doc. You can see I have collared these misfits. We missed dinner. Buster wouldn't happen to have any leftovers to feed us so's our bellies don't grumble through the night keeping everyone in the place awake?"

"Let me check on that." He left and returned quickly.

"You're in luck. Nine out of ten times there ain't a scrap left over. But here's you some biscuits and even a slather of bacon drippings. Go ahead and sit. I'll not be closing up for a while, yet."

We ate hungrily and washed it down with mugs of beer. And then after thanking Doc we went off to bed.

At breakfast we ate flapjacks, drank lots of coffee without saying a single word to each other, which was unusual. Most times I was the one who started the banter and the other two took their cues from me. But not on this day.

"I've been chewing on a distraction since we heard about Lucinda Poole. More hours go by and I just can't get shuck of it."

We had almost reached Pepper's stall. Mild snorts and whinnying told us that the burro had heard my voice.

"Well then we better hear about what this upset is, don't you think, Sam?"

"Well, just hear me out 'fore you say I'm foolish. First let's climb up to that outcropping yonder and sit. This story may take a while to tell."

We three climbed and sat down on some boulders, and then I began speaking. I skimmed through many parts and details but took time to paint a verbal picture of how Lucinda's songs had affected the wagon train travelers. I was wont to show my friends just how strong an impression the experience had been for me. The experience of Lucinda.

"So, now I find that very same young woman nearby. But she is thrashing about like a robin fallen from its nest, the fall of which has caused a wing to become bruised and useless.

"Somehow I must be an agent and come to her aid. Otherwise I fear my ignoring her plight would leave me feeling forever bereft. And now I think is the time to leap or be consumed."

Sam and Otis were more than a little bit stunned. Each had his own opinions of what was to come.

The gist of what needed to happen seemed a matter of sorting through some details. Any solution should be given consideration as well as mutual agreement.

"Way I see it, we maybe have a month or so before moving

up to the cabin for the winter. For now so long as we can count on staying at Doc's we could just carry on as we have been.

"Sam and me working at the placer claims and you putting in hours at the Printer Boy. That way you would be able to give any off-hours to helping resolve your lady friend's predicament."

We sat and pondered.

The sun had been moving across the sky towards the noon hour. Whenever this high mountain sun stayed constant in brilliant blue skies it could beat the living tar out of you. Right about now me and my friends were sweaty and uncomfortably warm due to the layers of clothing we habitually wore.

"Guess I'll mosey on up to the Printer Boy. Maybe put in a few hours' worth of work. What you think you'll do to pass the afternoon, boys?"

"Probably head over to Doc's and make sure he's got room for us for some days. Me, I'm going for a bath and see about getting my clothes washed. I might be able to talk Sam here into doing something likewise."

"Not me. I just bought a tub not a month ago. Won't be a 'needing to get all wet and soapy for at least another month. Maybe one of the days before we head back to the cabin."

Suddenly.

"You hear that racket coming from somewhere down the Gulch? Sounds like something crashing. Hey, I smell smoke!" Said an alarmed Otis.

We hightailed it fast as possible down the hillside to the road and squinted toward the distant haze. Then without stopping we ran fast as we could towards Doc's. Flames were leaping from an adjacent building and men were running every which way.

Everyone knew what a fire could do in no time at all. Burn down every single building without bias.

Buckets. Miners darted into buildings to procure some. A man ran down to the creek and filled a bucket. In quick order this water was thrown on the fire. Two men, then dozens more slid down the banks and filled buckets. They ran at break-neck speed from stream to fire, tossing water then returning for more. Even so, the fire was quickly getting away from them.

In short order it was noted that a bucket brigade to and from the nearby creek was the way to organize.

Two lines had become three as Otis, Sam and me joined the ranks of desperate men. In no time our trousers were soaked, our hands and fingers cramped. Our throats raw from breathing in the thick smoke.

The labor was non-stop and intense. Several hours passed before the men, including me and my friends, got control of the conflagration.

But not before it had destroyed a saloon and a boarding house, as well as the brothel in the tented lean-to. All this loss, in addition to the gambling hall where the fire had first started.

No lives had been lost.

Doc's boarding house was upwind and so was spared.

Smithson's, a ways down was not consumed, but the outer walls got scorched.

The air was acrid with black, oily smoke and the road had turned into a muddy quagmire mostly in front of the burned buildings.

Just now some hens from the small tented lean-to, now incinerated, joined the soiled doves from Madam Red Stockings place and began serving soup and bread from tables that the miners hustled to set up for this purpose.

And the fallen angels tirelessly fed the crowds throughout the dusky evening. They also provided pails of soapy water; so that any man who wanted the grime wiped from his face could dip a rag and have a scrub.

A couple of saloons rolled out barrels of beer.

The earlier atmosphere charged with a frenzy of commotion now changed to one of relieved revelling. Bottles of whiskey were procured from generous saloon keepers and passed from person to person.

Before the night was done men dropped wherever they fell from drunkenness. It was a comical scene to behold if one had a callous sense of humor.

The three of us managed to stagger into Doc's and later thanked him for steering us toward our beds.

No one knew how the fire started. A smoldering cigar? An overturned lantern? An act of God?

For a brief time there was talk of forming a Volunteer Fire Department but no man stepped forward to do the actual organizing.

The citizens of Oro City were doubtless shaken by the event but within a week or so the fire was relegated to the back of people's minds. And daily life resumed in the Gulch.

Millie was proving herself to be indispensable regarding Lucinda's recovery.

As a matter of fact, a few days after the fire as I was heading up to the Printer Boy, Isabelle stepped outside the school readying to ring the school bell.

"Morning to you, Miss Laughlin."

"Hello, Jasper. How are you this fine day?"

"Oh I can't complain when every day in the Gulch seems to be a display of beauteous nature in full display. May I inquire after the well-being of Lucinda?"

"Each day has its successes along with its setbacks. But Millie Abbot has been quite effective with my friend for these past several days. It does seem that each time I stop by to see Lucinda she appears a bit more improved."

"I await that day when she will again step outside of a morning and greet life with eagerness and resolve." I said with much sentiment.

"You have proved yourself a loyal and steadfast admirer. I plan to paint you in a favorable light when she is once again well. My friend should be told of your caring nature."

"Hearing you say this brightens the day. My pards and me are staying here in the Gulch until we get the first walloping of snow."

"Many miners light out as soon as winter comes. Where will you go? Maybe on down to Denver City?"

"No, Ma'am. We been a' buildin' a cabin in the hills north of here. Not too far. Plan to spend the winter months up there and then come back to work in the spring."

"Oh my. Well now I see my students making their way to the schoolhouse. Nice to see you, Mr. Gratz. Good day."

"Ma'am." And I doffed my hat.

Once again I busied myself with sharpening steel bits, six had piled up since I was last at work. And when next I looked up the morning was sliding into afternoon. I took a break and sat on the bench where once a stoic Lucinda had allowed me to yank out her tooth.

From this perspective I gazed down the length of the Gulch and across the wide expanse toward the majestic peaks to the west. Whenever I took the time to stop and contemplate the surroundings a feeling of contented resolve to remain in Oro well into the future flooded my heart.

Thoughts of Pepper standing in his stall intruded into my reverie and so I took off the heavy apron and headed back towards the town.

"Hidey ho, burro! I see your pails are filled with oats and water. Here be a treat I've been saving for you." And placed my cupped hand with apple wedges under Pepper's muzzle.

The beast gobbled the apple greedily. Still chewing he waggled his head and a snort issued forth.

"I see you ain't learned no manners in the last day or two. But at least you don't have hind leg kicks nor skunk smell, so that's an improvement. We'll be going over to the cabin maybe tomorrow to check on things so there's something to look forward to, eh?"

I gave Pepper an affectionate rubbing over his bristly head before I turned to walk down the dusty rutted road.

I needed some grooming. My light beard was looking scraggly and my clothes gave off an unpleasant rankness. So I turned into the building which offered baths and shaves. The latter was a recent offering.

Millie Abbot gave a furtive look in both directions before leaving Madam Red Stockings' building. As she walked briskly up to Lucinda's, she reminded herself that because she was not sharing her charge's cramped quarters of late, her lodging was a problem. So until a change could be arranged, she must remain on guard. Noone must know that she has been residing in a brothel, whether out of necessity or not.

Days were becoming less wearisome as Millie's patient continued to improve. Lately the dosage of laudanum was a fraction of a capful, in fact, less than a few drops on the tongue at night.

At the moment the young woman with auburn curls peeking out around her face lifted off her bonnet and set it down on the table along with her shawl.

"My dear Lucinda, you have already dressed for the day! I have brought you a breakfast of cornbread and coffee. Sit down here by the window and I'll brush out your hair."

"Good morning, Millie. I believe that last night was the soundest rest for me in a long, long time. And right at this moment I am happy and strong, very nearly filled with a sense of well-being."

"Nothing gives me more pleasure than hearing you speak so. You have been very brave for so long, and your positive willpower has served you time and again. When Miss Isabelle and Mrs. Tabor come here to visit it is my feeling that you will display an optimistic outlook."

"What does this mean, Millie? I'm not sure I'm completely healed and ready to be out once again among people. I am shaky."

"Your friends only want to see the new and improved you. Of course you feel some doubts. After all, you have suffered from quite an ordeal. Fighting the demon narcotic as you have done is highly admirable."

"Oh Millie, I'd give anything never to have tasted the stuff in the first place."

"Well you know that what's done is done, Lucinda. No one can go back and undo past happenings. Rather, we must shake off the dust of the crooked road and set our footsteps back upon the straight path."

"You are very wise for one so young. I am grateful to have you as a guide leading me through dark passages and onto the safer realms beyond. I shall always be in your debt. You are the best friend and nurse a girl could ever hope to have.

"And Millie, since this day is so bright and positive feeling I remember you once saying that one day you would share your story with me. After all I know next to nothing of your past and heaven knows you know all about my own."

"You are right. I once did make such an offer. But let's go outdoors, maybe to the creek bank where on such a fine day we will be surrounded by warmth and beauty of sound and sight."

So they tied on bonnets, wrapped shawls about their shoulders although with the soft fine breeze they would be warm enough without such. The two scooted down the nearby embankment. Settling on some good sized boulders as songs of robins and buzzing insects mingled with the soft sunshine, Millie began to talk.

"I was brought up on a hard-scrabble farm the oldest of several children. Me mam and pap married me off to a no-account when I was but fourteen."

She told of her husband's death which had had very little impact on her. And next described her infant daughter's sickness, death, and burial which had mattered greatly and had left her bereft.

Finally she described life within those sordid walls of Madam Red Stockings. She concluded with an emphatic statement that as yet she had had no occasion of a demeaning nature with men.

"It was the good Mrs. Tabor who rescued me at the final

hour so that I could exchange whoring for a ministry of nursing. And so it is that I came to you."

Lucinda swiped tears from her cheeks and drew in a deep breath.

She was most affected by Millie's narration. It struck her that the pain and agony which life afforded countless numbers of women in this time and place was for them a burden beyond endurance and wrought with unbearable sorrow.

For the unfortunate life lurched into gloom and inevitable doom.

For the fortunate life remained scratching and grasping for daily survival.

"I have an idea that will offer you a life free of Madam Red Stockings and her sordid bordello." Said Lucinda to her friend.

That same evening while eating rabbit stew me, Otis, and Sam mulled over some near future plans.

"Tell you what, Jasper. Me and Sam have been thinking to join the work crews who've been digging that ditch that's to bring forth water from Evans Gulch into this here gulch."

"Sam hill, Boys! Just when did this idea come into play? I don't like to meddle but have you ironed out the wrinkles of the plan? Or is it to be caution to the wind and damned the outcome?"

"Didn't think to get you so riled. There's nothing to stop us jumping in and out of the work. Just could be steady-like jobs for us until it gets closer to winter." Said Sam, and he added, "Help shore up our stockpile for the wintry months ahead."

Otis said, "No work in rewashing. That's finished until there be some water coming in. That's a fact."

"Well. Took me by surprise is all. I am aware that you both have lived through winter snow and cold up here and can grasp the truth of just how long we could be cut off from Oro. Supplies are all important, I do agree."

And so for the next few weeks or more depending on the weather we three men worked, ate, slept and worked some more.

Every day I took time to tie a lead onto Pepper and exercise him. I worked out puzzlements by speaking aloud to my burro. Matter of fact, this was sound therapy and presumably soothed the both of us.

Indeed, I looked on Pepper as a confidant. So many thoughts and musings about Lucinda could be aired and no one the wiser.

Now came the time for Lucinda to appear before the public. She was grateful to have an understanding manager in Mr. Smithson.

"So Miss Poole, I pray you are fully recovered from the sickness and ailments of the past month?"

"Yes I am indeed. And quite anxious to begin performing. I would like to have my dear friend, Millie Abbot join me during performances, as I have need of a second pair of hands to turn the music pages."

"Well I'm not agreeable to paying double wages until I see how the men respond to this Millie Abbot."

"Yes, of course, Mr. Smithson."

She had not been forthcoming about the nature of her recent illness and so was confident that her secret would remain hidden from the folks in the Gulch.

She donned her performance outfit, dressed her hair, and set off down the dusty road which was full of noise and the clamor of men looking for any means that might offer relief from the long, hard days of mining.

A Friend is Gone

Just as she and Millie were nearing the entrance to the hall a runaway wagon with snorting and galloping horses in harness nearly ran them over. They both leaped toward the doorway and fell into the hall.

"Oh, how dreadful! How I am to keep my wits about me seems quite beyond comprehension." Lucinda thought to herself.

Millie took the event in her stride.

Mr. Smithson came to their aid with immediacy.

"Have you been injured, either of you?"

"No. I'm quite unhurt." They spoke as one.

"Someone must catch the runaway wagon before it does injury to others on the road." Said Millie.

"I'll see what can be done." And at this he walked into the street.

Lucinda peaked out the door to peer down the road. Sure enough the wagon had crashed a half mile down the way and dozens of folks were swarming around the accident site. She could make out no details from this distance.

Nearly an hour later she sat at the piano practicing the notes she needed for the first songs she planned to perform. Millie stood behind her, studying the music. Smithson came in and crossed over to them.

Lucinda looked up and peered at his face noting the consternation which creased his brow.

"I can see by your face that you bear sad news. Please do not spare us. We are not so delicate that we cannot take frankness."

"If you insist I will relate the incident. As the horses attempted to maneuver round a bend they ran over three men who had the bad luck of crossing from the creek at that very moment. Two have met their maker this day and the third is not far behind. It is a gruesome and bloody scene. One that not soon be forgot by me and other witnesses."

Lucinda felt much strengthened in her constitution and would not succumb to the vapors. So she thought for a moment and then drew in a deep breath before speaking.

"I feel that it would be in poor taste to fill the street with gaiety after such tragedy. Would you not agree, Millie?"

Smithson stood by silently contemplating this idea before speaking again. He took his watch from the chain that hung from his vest pocket and noted the hour.

"I appreciate your sentiments, Miss. However, what the folks need is some way to turn away from a tragedy and seek the means to lighten their outlook. Maybe if the pieces are chosen with a solemn and serene nature it would give comfort and solace."

And so this plan is what was agreed to.

The next morning while Millie was gathering her meager belongings from the brothel, Lucinda was speaking with Mrs.

Tabor in subdued tones when Isabelle entered the store.

Isabelle greeted them both and said, "I am overjoyed at your successes. Lucinda. You have shown such courage and bravery for all this long time! I am hoping that we may resume being in one another's company for our meals and walks."

"Oh my good friend. Yes, I would very much like to have the opportunity to visit with you and share our mealtimes again. A new and happy development regards Millie. She is no longer under the shadow of the bordello. We will arrange some new dwelling and she will work side by side with me in the Hall."

"Oh, Lucinda! A most wonderful change of fortune for her." Said Isabelle, and Mrs. Tabor nodded most enthusiastically.

"What do you know of those ill-fated men who were overrun by the runaway horses yesterday evening? Has anyone come forth with their identities?" Asked Lucinda.

Before speaking Mrs. Tabor looked ill at ease. "I had information regarding one victim from a confidant late last night. Samuel Bakke, a cousin of Jasper Gratz. The others are unknown to me at this time. Lucinda, you are an acquaintance of Jasper if memory serves."

Lucinda paled and gasped. "Oh no! Dreadful, dreadful news!"

Once news of the tragedy reached me up at the Printer Boy the Miners' Committee had already moved the ill-fated victims into a tent which in future was meant to be yet another gaming hall.

Soon Otis and me were standing around the space, our hands in pockets with sorrowful, befuddled faces, not knowing what to do with our eyes and feet. I used the tail end of my flannel shirt to keep tears from dripping into my collar. Someone asked did we want to have a look at Sam.

So we each peered under the blanket. Sam didn't look so awful bad considering he'd just been trampled to death.

"Jasper, I am sore distressed by the loss of our mate. Sam and I had just checked in our tools at Tom Starr's shed after working on the ditch. I held back so as to review some details for the digging project and Sam went on ahead. I heard the crash and the screaming horses and ran up to the road. Don't like to say what the horrible scene looked like." He shuffled his feet and coughed into his neckerchief before asking, "What think you about where his remains be buried?"

"Oh, Otis. I'm full of such sorrow and grief. I don't think my addled brain can organize a plan quite yet. I will need the day and night to calm my senses. What say you?"

"What always seems a reliable source to go to is Mrs. Tabor. Or might could be Doc would have some idea what direction we might take. I can't think square about this right now, either. Let's head up to Doc's."

Once seated Doc came over and sat with us. Buster walked up, dingy rag draped over his arm and asked did we want the evening's fare served. None of us was interested in food but Doc said to bring some beers.

"Don't have any smart words to soothe such sorrows." Said Doc.

'Didn't think anything like this would happen. Just didn't see it coming." I said, shaking my head and tapping the table top with my fingers.

Otis drew in a ragged breath and seemed to shrink deeper into himself. He could not remember feeling such deep sorrow. At least not for a long, long time.

Not since leaving his family's homestead back in Ohio. He didn't dwell on the hardscrabble life of his growing up years nor of the loss of two tiny sisters, neither of whom had lasted more than a week on this earth. He didn't see much point in living his past life more than once.

And so after a night filled with grief-laden hours the day dawned cloudy and wet. Unusual for this time of the early fall season. It seemed that the very heavens were desolate.

Me and Otis walked up to Tabor's store after sipping Doc's coffee. We had both passed on the flapjacks. No appetites.

Mrs. T. ushered us over to a quiet corner and bade us sit on empty whiskey barrels. After she helped a handful of customers, she then set the "closed" sign in the front door window.

"Oh, my friends. I am much shaken by our loss. Sam was a good solid citizen of Oro City. I dare say that he will be missed by many in these parts. Once you have inked a letter to notify those in Germany hand it to me to be posted. Father Dyer is due any day to retrieve the mailbags."

"Thanks, Ma'am. Jasper and me would sure like your in-put as to how we can manage a meaningful send off for Sam."

"Let me think on it for a spell, Otis, Jasper. Would you stop on by in a few hours?"

As us two stepped from the store a heavy rain lashed out from leaden skies. Wind tore through the Gulch with the ferocity of a tempest. We ran over to Pepper's stall and found the burro just now working up to brandish his temper.

"Hey, now ol' boy. Just try to calm yourself. No need to add to the fury of the storm with your stomps and screams. I'll stay right here by you till the worst of it has played out." I used a soothing tone and kept my hands moving over the bristly fur on his back and head.

Pepper seemed to appreciate the attention as always. He rubbed his nose on my arm and eventually rested his whole head on my cupped and outstretched hands. I took as much comfort from this animal as the burro did from me.

The downpour did not let up for a good half hour. The wind continued wailing and blowing dirt and debris for much longer, though, so me and Otis remained standing under the protection of the stable roof.

When once the storm abated and the heavy clouds had blown off toward the western peaks we stepped back over to the road. A gushing stream along with some good sized rocks and tree limbs now covered the dirt road.

"Strange doin's is all I can say. But the air smells sweet and fresh." Said Otis taking in deep drafts. "Always some good comes out of upheaval. Not meaning that there's a silver lining by Sam's passing. I can't imagine life here without our pard." He concluded.

Samuel Bakke's burial was a quiet affair. His grave was on

the south bank of the stream, a slight distance from Tom Starr's property. The mourners were fewer than a dozen. Friends in the Gulch and some miners he'd worked with on the placers. In these times death was a stealthy thief and grieving was a luxury most could not afford to squander time on.

After volunteering for a day to help clear the detritus from the road which the storm had left in its wake, me and Otis decided without deliberation to gather supplies into our cart so as to trek back over to the cabin in short order.

Pepper presented a somber bearing as if displaying his mourning for the absent Sam. Needless to say I was always grateful for any respite from this quarter.

Otis and me approached our cabin on heightened alert taking note of any disturbance in the surrounds.

We unloaded the cart and unharnessed Pepper before hobbling him in his small lean-to.

We didn't take time to reflect on the extra bedstead in the main room.

Otis made a fire in the yard ring and I filled a kettle at the stream so we could have coffee. Then we sat down on the yard logs and attempted to relax.

"We should hike up to Jake's and give him the news about Sam."

Why don't you go on without me, Otis? Maybe bring Jake back with you so's we might have a sort of wake."

Otis agreed. And within an hour he returned with Jake in tow.

In due time us men threw out our coffee and filled cups with whiskey from Jake's jug.

As the level of drink in the jug decreased the volume of loudness brought forth by the mourners increased.

"It sure is soothing to have a friend to share stories about Sam. It takes the sting out of our keening. Don't it, Jasper?"

Just at this moment the men heard two things. First some people on horseback moving through the trees, slowly.

And second, Pepper starting up his braying squeals while stomping and kicking at his lean-to supports.

We looked up as a band of five or six Utes on fine looking ponies ambled up to the cabin yard. I rose slowly from my log and nodded to the newcomers, and then I made my careful way over to Pepper and spoke to the burro about not becoming nervous. Also, I smoothed the bristled fur on his flanks and then turned back to see what was up with the Utes.

After some hand motions and simple imitations it was understood that the band of natives was a hunting party intending no harm. As I recalled my encounter with such after leaving Auraria at the edge of the foothills, a mutual greeting was all that was warranted.

The Utes turned their mounts in a northerly direction and then were gone.

"Hey ya, Jake, you think your cabin might be molested by those fellows?"

"Nah. I've seen Utes now and again and they feign only curiosity much the same as I do. They never appear menacing, but always just go on about their business."

"Yeah. Some of the miners in Oro City are much more rowdy and dangerous." I said, seemingly less aggrieved than Otis, who hadn't spoken since the episode began.

"I'm more bothered by the suddenness of their arrival than any mal-intent that might come with it." Said Otis. "If they'd approach with more fanfare it would be less unsettling."

"Uh huh. But that's not their way. Their way is to be stealthy." Said Jake.

He soon took his leave and promised to see us once more whenever we came back from the Gulch.

"How many days ya reckon we'll stick around here, Jasper, before heading back?"

The effects of the whiskey had dissipated in me within the last hour, what with Ute hunters and an upset Pepper. So now I shrugged my shoulders and paced the yard before responding.

"A few. I need the serenity of the woods, the drone of insects and birdsong before going back to the boisterous Gulch. That suit you?"

Otis grunted in the affirmative and poked up the fire in the pit.

"Might mix us up some biscuits for supper since we have us this fire goin'. How about some of that jerky we have stored in the cave up yonder?"

"All sounds good to me, Jasper. I'll fix the biscuits while's you see about the meat."

Two of us were ever compatible having been together these long months. It was simply a hole in each of our hearts left behind by Sam that filled us with a seeping sadness.

Nighttime came on softly and sounds of woodland creatures foraging for food lulled us both until at last we dropped onto our beds inside the cabin and slept.

Back in the Gulch once more I lunged into my work greasing crankshaft parts and sharpening picks and drill bits. There was never a shortage of tasks for a blacksmith. I worked non-stop until Judson interrupted me.

"You won't hold out for too long at the pace you been goin'. Here, have a chunk of cornbread and a cup of water. Else we'll be needing to find you a pallet in the sick tent."

"Thanks for sharing your lunch. I hadn't thought to bring anything along today. I have been preoccupied with the loss of my friend, Sam. And I have to write a letter to his people back in Aachen, Germany. I don't write too good and I guess I'll just have to pen the simple facts and send it along."

"Yep. That was a fearsome piece of frightful luck. Sometimes a man's time is just up. No way to reason it."

"Well it's a darn shame Sam had to be the one to go. Guess I'll make this a short day. I'm running on empty. I'll come back up and start an early shift tomorrow, if that suits?"

"You bet, Jasper. Tip a few for me."

I sauntered along the road until I came to Lucinda's boarding house. I slowed down and studied the window on the second floor which I surmised was her room. As chance would have it the curtain pulled back and the face of an angel peered out at me.

Lucinda waved slowly and then vanished.

"Hello, Mr. Gratz." She said, coming onto the dusty road near to where I stood.

Finding myself speechless I simply nodded.

Lucinda showed some spark and went ahead addressing me. "I extend my deepest sympathies for your loss of Samuel. It was the cruelest of tragedies. Many people in the Gulch thought highly of him. He will be sorely missed."

At last finding my voice I said, "Otis and me are much distressed by Sam's passing. He was our prized partner."

I was quite uneasy and jittery in her company. Especially because of the unexpectedness of the encounter. I kept foolishly shuffling my feet and wiping away nonexistent sweat from brow and neck with a grimed bandana.

Lucinda appeared cool and composed as she slowly waved a fan in front of her face.

"He was from your own home place in Germany is what people say. Is this true, Mr. Gratz?"

"Yes, Ma'am, true enough. Although, I didn't know Sam in my growing up years. In fact, didn't know him at all before meeting him here in Oro City. Otis and me came across him one day shortly after arriving in the Gulch and from that time on called him friend."

Clearly I was so caught off balance by this chance encounter that I couldn't stop my feet from kicking at the rocky dirt of the road. I even bent down to pick up a yellowish stone and slowly tossed it back and forth in my hands.

"Is that a gold nugget you've got there, Mr. Gratz?" She kidded him.

"Wishful thinking. If it was gold why about 50 men would be swarming around here in five minutes flat." I took in a deep breath and said, "Would you kindly consider calling me Jasper, Ma'am?"

"I will absolutely use your Christian name, sir, only if you will cease in addressing me as Ma'am. I am Lucinda Poole. And it seems to me that once a person has yanked a rotten tooth from another's mouth each would then be on familiar footing with one another. At least friendly enough for first names."

"Miss Lucinda, I am at your service any time you have need for dentistry."

I knew I was embarrassing myself minute by minute. I just couldn't figure a way to untangle myself from my own buffoonery. But I blundered ahead in spite of myself.

"I must tell you that I clearly remember you from the wagon train which brought us from the east. I have clear recollections of your pretty voice floating over the nightly encampments. Your songs added succor and serenity to many a tired and weary folk."

"Well, I must say, Jasper! I am stunned by your memories of that time. Because I was widowed and bereft, I sang merely to ease my own tormented soul. To be told all these long months hence that I was of some comfort to my fellow travelers is truly astonishing. I must say that you are kind to share this with me."

At this I dropped the rock and rubbed my dusty hands on my trousers. I smiled, nodded, and doffed my hat.

"I'm looking forward to attending your performances at Smithson's Hall, Miss Lucinda. I hope to arrive early so as to find a front row seat."

"I intend to resume performances tomorrow evening, Jasper. And by way of thanking you for ending my dental torment, a payment if you will - a place will be reserved for you each evening I'm at the Hall. And thank you for this lovely chance meeting. It has truly been a pleasant happenstance. Good day."

"Many thanks and good day to you." My hammering heart was still humming away. I was beside myself with blissful happiness. Oh, lucky day!

Now I was on the lookout for Otis. I hadn't thought to ask my friend what work he'd had in mind for the day. My feet now took me to Doc's. Always a good bet when trying to find Otis and Sam. Um, Otis, just Otis.

"Seen Otis today?" I asked the serving man, Buster.

A grunt in the negative.

"Hmm? Where to look?" I thought to myself.

A mongrel dog came sniffing at my leg. I pushed it away and moved to the south edge of the road looking hard towards the placers. Lots of activity along the branches of creeks. Eventually I spotted Otis climbing the bank from way down by Tom Starr's place. So I sat on the top of the embankment to wait.

The din of digging and shoveling along with the voices of the miners filled the air. But it was noise that I somehow found comforting. Work. Prosperity.

"Hey yo, Jasper." Otis called out as he came near enough to be heard.

"Otis. What's going on down at Starr's?"

"Nothing much. Talk of a hanging. Looks as though another of the Reynold's Gang wandered into the Gulch yesterday. Couldn't keep his big mouth from boasting about how ruthless his gang once was. Someone alerted the Miners' Commission and before the night was over the fellow found himself bound hands and feet and dragged into a barn. The trial was earlier today. He'll be a 'swinging tonight."

"Reynold's Gang, huh? That bunch of outlaws worked over on the Buckskin side of Mosquito Pass? Robbed stages carrying the gold bound for Fairplay?"

"Yep. You remember rightly. Apparently this man is the only one hadn't yet been caught and killed or strung up. Now it's his turn to get a stretched neck. It's never a shame to see a blackguard get his come-uppance."

"How's about an early meal at Doc's and some whiskey drinking for a while afterwards. Otis?"

"Sounds good to me, but it don't sound like your ways, Jasper. Something happen to put some pluck in your activities?"

"Uh, yeah. Could be. I'll tell you about it while we're relaxing at Doc's."

And I did. But I waxed poetic for so long that Otis grew antsy and suggested that we take up conversing at a saloon bar. It wasn't conversing so much as it was someone talking and someone half-listening.

We two walked into a saloon three doors down from Doc's and stepped up to the bar. Only a handful of miners were in there.

"Hey, barkeep, how come so quiet in here?"

"They're all down at the hanging. Everyone wants to see this one swing. Rode with the Reynold's Gang, they say."

"Heard about this earlier. Completely slipped my mind. Ol' Jasper here had some important matters to parlay about. Took considerable time."

Just about then men in twos and threes started coming in. Lots of animated talk.

Otis asked one man, "Did the spectacle end with the usual fanfare?"

"Slippery cuss. Almost got free of his fetters just as the noose dropped over his head. He wouldn't of got free with so many laws around, though. Yep. He's a dead 'un now and good riddance."

Plenty of wound-up folks on the road as Otis and me made

our way back to Doc's.

"Be some boozed up men before the nights through, I reckon. Times like these I'm good and glad we have our beds at Doc's." Said Otis.

Over beans and cornbread the next morning I mentioned to Otis that Lucinda was going to perform at Smithson's that very night. I added that I meant to buy a bath and shave when my shortened shift was over.

"What does that mean? Shortened?" Asked Otis.

"Means I'm only working this morning. I don't want anything to interfere with me being at the Hall when Lucinda sings tonight."

"Oh, well. I guess I'll go a' digging the ditch for a few hours. I'm going to forgo the bath, though. Too much clean is not healthy, is what my ma always said. Boiling creek water was a big chore so I don't blame her for her point of view on the matter."

Then as he was walking away he said, "We'll meet at Doc's for supper, Jasper?"

I nodded yes and I started up the road.

I dropped by Pepper's stall to tie on a lead so's my burro can come along up to the forge. Once there I hobbled the animal and got to work. I talked to Pepper as I went about sharpening a pickax.

Later on after supper Otis and me find ourselves in front of Smithson's Hall. Seemed to be only a handful of men standing around with hands in pockets.

After a spell Smithson opened up the doors and bade us enter. We took the most advantageous seats on a bench real close to the piano.

"Might be we're sitting so close to the front, Jasper, we just might find ourselves breathing down the singer's back."

"I'll not worry over any such thing. 'Sides Lucinda saved these places for us particularly. Said she would."

And in came not one but two ladies in stylish dresses. I breathed in deeply and smiled when Lucinda turned her face towards me. She looked so pretty in a fancied up gown, not one to be worn every day but one decorated to dazzle a crowd of miners. It had some ribbons on the top part.

Otis was nudging me in the ribs as he gazed at the second gal. She too was decked out in a few ruffles and bows. She was a comely lass with dark red hair done up in curls, a bright complexion and small, much the size of Lucinda.

"Who's the lass with Lucinda?" He whispered near my ear.

"Shhh. Don't know. Find out later."

The Hall filled up within minutes. Boots drubbing the floors and miners stinking up the place rankled me some. A concert hall would be more suitable for this charming songbird. With the first notes struck on the piano box the men quieted down.

Otis and me sat engrossed, practically enraptured before the first song was finished.

I'm not certain of the names of the tunes. I recognized "Green Grow the Lilacs" from the wagon train, though.

Otis and me strode out to the road almost two hours later just ahead of the crowd. The evening had turned chilly. Mid-autumn not too awful far away.

"Thanks, Jasper, for bringing me along this night. I need to find out who the pretty redhead is. She hasn't been in Oro very long I don't think or one of us would have come across her. Don't you think?"

"Don't know, Otis. Can't think where she could put herself and not be seen. She was surefire seen tonight, though. I will tell you out and out that when I see Lucinda next I'll find out her name for you."

We were just outside a saloon that we frequented and non verbally agreed to enter. Stepping up to the bar Otis ordered two whiskeys. Once the drinks were served we threw them back and signaled for refills.

"I can't get my mind to move in any direction save for the beauty who stood next to your Lucinda. Can't think of a single female who's ever turned my head so utterly and fully. And instantly."

"You're not going to do something like fall in love, are you, Otis?"

"Can't think of myself in such a state, Jasper. But I mean to explore the notion first chance I get. Main thing though is finding out who she is, exactly."

We rarely lingered over more than a couple of drinks. So now we wandered in the direction of Doc's and bed.

Meanwhile after the final number Lucinda and Millie stood to the applause. Mr. Smithson motioned for them to meet with him after the Hall emptied.

"Well, Miss Poole and Miss Abbot, that was quite successful tonight! Before I pay wages to you, Miss Abbot, I'll wait and have you appear together one more time. See if the men continue to be stirred by a second performance." He continued, "Tomorrow evening, same time, Ladies?"

"Oh, yes, your proposal is quite sound." Said Lucinda. And Millie nodded enthusiastically.

The following evening rolled around on schedule. Lucinda and Millie were in their places at the piano box looking over the program selections.

"We will begin with 'O Shenandoah' and follow it with 'Sweet By and By' and next 'Wayfaring Stranger'. We'll sing 'Green Grow the Lilacs' and end with 'O Suzanna' and finally a medley of all including "Wildwood Flower."

"Um, Lucinda, what do you think of my joining in on the chorus of a song or two?"

"Oh, Millie, what a splendid idea! Sing whichever tunes you know tonight and in future we will rehearse and see what develops with some others."

At the end of the evening performance the miners clapped, stomped and yelled their approval. Al Smithson was over the moon.

Alas! The evening was tarnished when two false-hearted mining spectators began an altercation with some law abiding placer miners and before Smithson could throw them into the road blood was spilt. A bullet grazed the arm of one miner and the second miner was attempting to wrestle with the other two deviants.

As is common with such altercations in Oro City several of the crowd within pushed and prodded until the mayhem was in the middle of the road. The disreputable speculators were divested of their weapons and tied with ropes, hands and feet.

"Blackguards like you will shortly answer to the Mining Committee. But you'll sit where you are until those men can be summoned." Said a miner from Starr's crew.

"Oh, Lucinda, how dreadful! Maybe we should offer help to that wounded man."

"Of course you're right. Mr. Smithson, is there anything we can do to help?"

But Millie had already jumped to action. She said, "We must tie a cloth around the arm - keep it from bleeding overmuch."

Smithson hurried over with three bandanas he'd grabbed from a few onlookers. "Here. Use these."

Millie used skills she'd picked up mainly from the wagon train to tie a tourniquet around the man's arm. This stanched the flow of blood until the new doctor in Oro could be beckoned forth.

Finally after the turmoil eased up the young women were able to take their leave of the place.

Once outside in the fresh bracing night air the two gazed up at the night sky. Soft noises followed them as they walked. The creek bouncing over rocks and a fox calling to its mate somewhere in the trees.

"So many stars in the firmament and the moon is full to light us along our way. Oh, Millie, I just can't seem to keep from being addled by such violent events. I should think that my inner nature might have become stronger by now."

"Lucinda, this is a hard place. It is not a civilization for women. We struggle each day to maintain anything of grace and refinement. But we somehow manage to offer only a handful of soft moments to the men who come into the Hall for solace. Please don't become downhearted. You are well respected and held in high regard by all who come to hear your lovely voice."

But, Lucinda was discouraged in spite of her friend's heartfelt speech. She could feel herself slipping closer and nearer to that dark empty place which nothing could fill except the contents in the cobalt bottle. This is what she needed and wanted. Only this. And she would not be denied. As a matter of fact her stride quickened so that Millie had to work to stay abreast.

Millie had an inkling that something was stirring in her friend's mind. She hoped and prayed that it was not the fiendish drug rearing its ugly head. If this was the case she determined to deal with it however much time and strength it took.

"Maybe", she thought, "if I execute it carefully I can nip it in the bud."

Well, Lucinda was single-minded and would do what she must to ease her inner pain. She would convince Augusta Tabor that she must have it.

The two women climbed the stairs at the Holiday House and Lucinda was first to change out of her fancy clothes. They had a system which worked well so that the small shared space was roomier. One would dress or undress and the other would linger on the stairs waiting her turn.

On this occasion Millie called through the door that she felt like waiting by the creek and added that she would return shortly. Instead she ran quickly to Tabor's store, pounded on the locked door and told a sleepy Augusta that she needed the laudanum which they kept hidden behind the counter, and then ran back over to the HH.

Lucinda was just then descending the stairs although not dressed in nightclothes.

"I mean to take a walk by myself to soothe my racing thoughts, Millie."

"Oh, but I was hoping that we would keep to our routine and chat quietly until sleep comes to us. Please allow me a minute to change and then join me inside, Lucinda." Her rapid breathing from running made her sides heave.

"Oh, Millie. You've found me out, have you not? I saw you just now darting over to Augusta's store. Scheming to keep me from my medicine, the two of you. I just know you are." She said this, as tears began to overflow from her eyes.

Tucking an arm through Lucinda's Millie said, "I have so much affection for you, you know this well. I brought a portion with me that will get you past this damnable moment. Please come along, my dear, all will be better by and by."

A spoonful of the demonic elixir was all that was needed to put Lucinda into a deep untroubled slumber. Millie decided to hide the half-empty bottle inside one of her lace-up boots.

The next day showed nearly overcast skies which would portend rain later.

Millie dressed hurriedly and scooted across the road, handing off the bottle to Augusta who nodded sympathetically. Back in the room she sat on her bed and picked up a stocking which needed darning.

Nearly an hour later Lucinda awoke and stretched lavishly. She glanced at Millie and quite suddenly recalled the previous night.

They exchanged "good mornings" and Lucinda became withdrawn. Millie was having none of it and determined to ward off a breakdown with all the strength she possessed.

"Well, now, I know it isn't much but I saved the spoon from last night and it is well coated with the syrup. Here, lick it clean and then we'll take ourselves off to breakfast."

"A spoonful would be more satisfying. Let me see the bottle, Millie."

Millie breathed in and out deeply and said, "The bottle isn't in this room. I have it safely stored away. You know full well that this is the only reasonable strategy, my dear. We must stay vigilant or a spell will have you in its heartless clutches and rather than singing we'll be chasing."

"You mean chasing the demon away. I understand and I am beholden to you as to no other."

"After breakfast let's go to the schoolroom and have a nice visit with Isabelle." Lucinda said, as they walked toward the cook house.

Millie's mood was quite optimistic and she happily agreed to the break in routine. It seemed a favorable sign that Lucinda would not succumb to her addiction for now.

A short time later as they approached the schoolhouse Isabelle was just coming through the door.

"Oh my! What a lovely surprise. We have so much to catch up on that I don't see how we will satisfy ourselves in the short half hour before the school day commences. I have several topics of discourse so we'll begin now and sometime soon we'll take up again." Isabelle said, smiling broadly.

Lucinda and Isabelle exchanged news and Millie was content to listen and learn from their stories about goings on in Oro City. She wasn't the least bit intrusive and was happy to be filled with all manner of information past and present. When the first youngsters could be seen climbing the road to the schoolhouse Isabelle bade them goodbye and went over to ring the school bell. They all waved to one another.

"I'm pleased that you kept my confidences secret, Millie. I wish Isabelle to think that the tempest is behind me. She should be able to heap all her energies onto her students and not worry over her friend's burdens."

"You can always rest assured that your safety and well-being are my top priorities. I would never betray your confidence. I am your loyal friend."

"Thank you, Millie. I think I must go to see Augusta and

report that my feet are once more on solid ground. She has seen me through more than enough of these horrid episodes. And presently she will be told of my grateful heart for her generous patronage."

As they walked along Lucinda pointed up to a deep blue sky with huge white clouds piled high one atop another. The clouds might portend rain later but it was breathtakingly beautiful to gaze upon and for now made them feel a benediction.

When the ladies entered the Tabor store they were taken aback by the presence therein of Otis and me. We were busy purchasing bags of feed for Pepper. Turning toward the opening door we doffed our hats in unison and the ladies each nodded their greetings.

As I worked up the nerve to speak Otis blushed crimson beneath his beard. Neither of us felt at ease in the society of ladies, but I was less inhibited than Otis. After all I had had the good fortune of being in Lucinda's company previous times and though I felt I'd won no accolades for my wit and humor, I knew that I hadn't blundered overmuch.

"Miss Poole, how do you do on this fine day?" I said, addressing her more formally while inching toward the very object of my affections.

"I am quite well, thank you. May I introduce a dear friend and fellow performer, Miss Millie Abbot?"

"How do, Miss? I am Jasper Gratz and this is my partner, Otis Walls. Otis, you do recognize both Miss Poole and Miss Abbot, from the performance Hall." And I give my friend a subtle arm nudge.

"How do?" Barely audibly spoken. Otis shuffled his feet and slowly spun his hat round and round with sweaty hands. His innards were gripped by terror. Frankly he looked like he'd rather be facing a grizzly than to be in the presence of these fair damsels.

"May I say to each of you that we enjoyed your program last night immensely? Although in regard to the unfortunate events which ended in bloodshed, all that might be said is that such violence happens in any mining camp. Not just in Oro. But we worried for your safety." I was now within touching range of Lucinda as I spoke. But of course I practiced discrete restraint.

"While living these many months in Oro I can assure you, Mr. Gratz, that if one is to survive the rigors of life here one must become accustomed to all manner of things mean and rough. And by the way, Mr. Smithson is my guardian while I am in the Hall. And now Miss Abbot has his protection as well. So please not to worry."

Turning toward the counter she said, "Mrs. Tabor, I will no longer keep you from your customers but this afternoon before our program I will stop back by, if that suits. I have a small matter to impart." And so Lucinda bade farewell to all and took Millie by the arm as they departed.

Augusta Tabor shrugged taking the entire event in her stride. She was by nature a philosophical thinker. What would be would be.

As for me and Otis, we silently walked to the corral carrying the feed bags. Pepper was offered a piece of biscuit left from breakfast. The burro softly snorted and nodded his head slowly with an air of thanks. I then took time to clean out the stall.

In time us friends began bantering back and forth about the encounter that had just occurred with the ladies.

Otis offered this point of view. "Millie is a handsome slip of a thing. And she doesn't talk overly much. I find this quite agreeable in a female."

"Well, good thing, Otis, 'cause you brayed like a pack of burros giving no one else a chance to jump in and help with the back and forth talk. So how exactly could Millie put in her two cents worth?"

"No need to rib me, Jasper. I feel a proper fool as it is. I get so empty of words with females that I can't squeeze a single one past my lips. Never mind words, my head empties out 'til I'm completely bone dry. Guess I just haven't been around the fair gender enough to do much better."

"Way I see it, you can get schooled in conversing easy enough. Not by me. I'm no one's idea of a gallant. But maybe the schoolmarm could be of some help. I know her a little from when I pulled Lucinda's tooth and had to carry her home. Miss Isabelle scolded me for doing such a thing but afterwards I set her straight by explaining the necessity of being so familiar. And now we exchange pleasantries when we pass each other on the road."

We left the corral and went down towards the boarding hall to see Doc. Just before entering, though, Otis said, "Let me think on it. Don't be going off with any plan before I nod my go ahead."

I conceded. While eating a savory venison stew supper we both agreed that we needed to go to our cabin one day soon. We'd been here in Oro for well over a week and didn't think our cabin should be left unattended for overly long spells.

We decided to trek to the cabin the following day but I told Otis I'd look in on the schoolmarm and see about lessons in the fine art of conversing before we'd set off.

On the way up the trail I had Jasper on his rope and we were all of us enjoying the last of greenery on trees. It would be less than a month before the aspen leaves would become part of a soft mattress along with the pine needles. Suddenly the wind picked up considerably and blew each of our hats off.

I had a relaxed hold on Pepper's rope and he easily yanked it out of my grip, jolting me off guard as he took a notion to give chase. The hats were whirling and flipping from sage bush to willow clump and my animal was behaving like a complete jackass. Bucking and leaping over stumps and downed logs.

Of course Otis and me leaped into action. Otis went after the hats while I attempted to get hold of Jasper's harness. I took a tumble into a wild rose bush just as Pepper got his teeth on one of the hats. The rose thorns scratched up my face but in my fury I leaped forward and managed to grab hold of the trailing rope.

My hands were shaking and my breath laboring as I said, "I do not like you. You're unhelpful and undisciplined. You may think you can go your own way, but for one thing you're too lazy to obtain your own feed. First chance I get I'm selling you to some miner in Oro City who doesn't know you. And I'll use the profits to purchase me a less foolish animal."

I had scratches on my face and hands and when Otis caught up he offered me my hat and I handed him his own.

"By the looks of your face your beast has once again put you in harm's way, I fear, Jasper. Could be he spends his time over in his corral thinking up mischief. He sure has a knack for it."

"At the moment I'm too perturbed to think civil thoughts. He seems to bedevil me every chance he gets." And I yanked the hat down so hard it covered my ears.

Looking at his own hat Otis said, "Well, he managed to put his teeth deep into the brim of this here hat and now it looks ratty and tattered. I think I heard you threaten to sell him as I came astride and if so some money from the sale might be spent on a new hat for me. What say you to this, Jasper?"

All I could manage was a grunt.

We spent the better part of three days doing tasks around the place.

Lucinda and Millie ate their lunch and then returned to Tabor's store. They each felt a deep fondness for Augusta, and Lucinda walked over to her with outstretched arms.

"Oh, my dear Augusta, you have stepped in to act as my champion once again. I just wanted to thank you and personally tell you how life-saving your helpful choices have been, and on more than one occasion."

Augusta, holding Lucinda's hands in her own, spoke

affectionately. "I am a loyal and faithful friend. I will always be your ally. And because I have seen this particular narcotic devalue and even destroy good people before, I am determined to use all of my resources to keep you from tumbling into the abyss. Sometimes it takes many intercessions before one can experience complete success."

Millie chimed in, "As for myself, Augusta, it pleasures me to say that you have proven to be a worthy advocate. Whenever I need assistance you are most likely within reach."

Just then a freight driver cracked his whip over the backs of two mules as he pulled his wagon to the front of the store. Both Millie and Lucinda startled as it sounded like a shotgun blast.

"Alas, a loud whip crack often sounds like a gunshot, but both of you go along now and be of good resolve. And remember, I am always here."

"Let's go to our room and rest so that we'll be fresh for tonight". Said Lucinda.

As evening was upon the ladies they walked along the dusty, rutted road to have their supper.

Looking to the not so distant western peaks they noted that dark clouds obscured them. Weather was moving in.

"Look, Millie. We will be getting rain during the night."

"Maybe we should end our performance early so that we won't get soaked walking back up."

"Oh, let's wait and watch. I hate to shorten the program. The men need our music to lighten their daily drudgery at the placers." Said Lucinda.

The performance hall was jam packed. Every bench and standing place was occupied. The room smelled of the dirt and sweat each miner was shrouded in. The two ladies granted that the men had little opportunity to bathe after a day's work especially if their time allotted the choice of either a tub or a fine evening of entertainment. So the stench would be ignored and the audience would be appreciated.

The pleasurable evening ended. Millie and Lucinda walked as fast as they could so as to reach the Holiday House before the skies erupted. They were tucked into bed with blankets and shawls but rather than thunder and lightning the skies filled with fat snowflakes.

The following morning two inches of snow covered the ground. The high peaks to the west were winter white. Every person in Oro felt cheated out of some weeks of pleasant weather. After all the aspen leaves hadn't had their moment of glorious gold yet.

Instead some branches broke under the weight of the snow. The Gulch creeks were prematurely coated with ice. People hustled from building to building in the chilly air. And the snow kept up throughout the day. The noise on the gulch road was somewhat silenced.

On the second day the weather changed back to warmer in Oro City.

"Well. So this is an introduction to the snows of winter, eh, Otis?"

"Yep. A reminder that if a man's not made necessary preparations by now, he's missed his window of opportune."

"Guess we should wait a day or two for this here weather to clear before we go on back into Oro." I said.

"Hey Pepper. Seems like you're a' doing okay here in your snug lean-to. Don't mind the snow, do ya?" I said this yesterday just before the skies were full on snowing.

And so I was able to rest easy knowing Pepper was well set up. Early days we'd built a covered storage bin so his grain was readily accessible to human hands, but impossible for critters, large or small, to bust into. The water bucket still posed a problem, however. Have to work on this.

We hadn't planned to use the inside fireplace for a while yet. But the morning's coldness suggested we go ahead now and put it to use. First I needed to check Pepper's water bucket. Make sure it didn't freeze. Nope.

It didn't take long for the coffee to boil and I stirred up some flapjacks. Otis dug deep into the goods stacked on the shelves and finally found the jar of molasses.

Because of this we agree to use some hours rearranging the stores on the shelves so that items needed most often were more accessible.

There was a deck of cards on a shelf and so to while away the hours we played some simple and basic games of poker. Otis schooled me as we moved from game to game. I had had very little exposure to any sort of card playing so my pard spent a goodly amount of time showing me what was what.

A two night sleep-over is what the snow warranted.

On the second morning we boiled some coffee and ate warmed over flapjacks before heading off. As we hiked along we looked toward the west and noticed that the high peaks above the timberline were completely white.

The forest ground here about was wet and soggy with clumps of snow all around but already melted off the trail which we always used. The breezes were warming and the trek was pleasant enough. Bird song and small critter chatter followed us all the way to the Gulch.

"Hey, Otis, what in the Sam hill is all the ruckus down there by the creek?"

"Just got here myself, Jasper. Give me a short minute to try and figure it out." He paused and peered. "From what I can tell looks like some ornery cuss has been causing a commotion."

"Let's put Pepper in the stable and head over to Doc's."

No one was about the place except Buster who was clearing up after the breakfast crowd.

"Say, Buster, what's doing down by the placers?"

"Some un was a hollering about claim jumpers. But that's all's I know."

One of the crimes in mining areas occurred when swindlers came along hoping to take a working placer claim away from the rightful owner. Stealing property, in other words.

"Why don't we hot-foot it over to Tom Starr's place and get the low-down?" Said Otis.

A good sized cluster of miners was gathered around one of Starr's out-buildings. And right there in the midst of the mob were two scruffy faced no-accounts tied up hands and feet.

Next thing we knew the offenders were being dragged over to the barn-like structure where the Miners' Committee was ready to hold court. In no time at all the villains had been tried and found guilty of claim jumping.

And that was a hanging offense.

A scaffold stood permanently ready and the two would be hung at sundown.

"Claim jumpers are a wily lot, wouldn't you say, Otis?

"I'd say worse than that about them. They'd as soon use their thieving ways than do an honest day's labor. Why they'd multiply like vermin if they weren't apprehended, so that kind of behavior is not ever tolerated in any camp."

After watching all this disturbance at the creek we struck out for Doc's and some midday repast. No one hardly stopped in during the day but we hoped to maybe be offered breakfast leftovers. Just now Doc was sweeping dust from the entrance.

"Hi ya, Doc. What's the latest blather? We know about the claim jumpers. Blackguards, that kind." Otis said, entering the place with me on his heels.

"Blackguards is 'xactly right. I can't hardly stomach them no how. A decent man tries every which way to get by on his labors and before ya know here comes along some villain to rob him." Doc put his broom away before going on. "What can I do you boys for? Just getting back from your cabin?"

"All that claim jumping ruckus must've made us hungry. You think Buster might have something put back from breakfast?"

"Let me go ask him, Otis. You both just have a seat here, be right back."

Time we settled ourselves he returned with a plate in each hand.

"You're in luck. Here's some bacon and biscuits that might still be eatable."

"Say Doc, is the two ladies still doing their singing show at Smithson's some of these nights?"

"Far as I can tell from the miners' talking at mealtimes. They sure do think highly of that entertainment, I'd say, Friends."

We ate the food and swigged our beer and chatted some more with Doc before taking to the Gulch road.

"What say we amble on up to the schoolhouse and see if Miss Laughlin might be around to school me some?"

"Don't think she'd avail herself in the middle of the day, Otis. But it wouldn't hurt nothing to give it a try."

Otis was wearing his hat low on his forehead so I couldn't tell if he was truly smiling or frowning.

We walked up to the schoolroom door and pushed it open real quiet-like.

"What's this? No one here?"

"Don't fret, Otis. Got to be some reason or t'other. Let's circle around to the back. I think that Miss L. lives right here at the schoolhouse. She might be in her rooms now."

"Hello, gentlemen. I thought I heard some talking out front here."

"Hello, Ma'am. Do you have a holiday and so no school?"

She gives us a friendly nod while bending to yank some weeds from the dirt walkway.

"Jasper and Otis, is it? The students don't come on Saturday and Sunday. That's why the building is empty and mercifully quiet."

"Oh. We didn't think of that. We've been up to our cabin but being back in Oro for now thought we might inquire if you'd be willing to school Otis here in some social niceties with ladies?"

Otis' whole face turned bright red with self-consciousness. I felt right sorry for my pard. But then …

"I have some time this afternoon, Otis. If you'd care to sit in my classroom we could work there."

"Um, that would be just fine, just fine."

"I believe I'll walk on up to my forge and get a start on some sharpening while you're busy this way."

Isabelle blanched. "No, that will not do. It would not be respectable to be alone with a man and no chaperone." But she thought for a minute and went on. "We could sit outside here, I guess. No one much comes this high up the road on a Saturday. Would that be suitable, Otis?"

He looked as if he might back out of the whole arrangement, so I tried to give him some encouragement.

"I do believe that Miss Laughlin is right about no one bothering or interrupting you while you worked. What say you, Otis?"

"Well, I'm not so sure, but I guess I might give it a try. Don't see as it would hurt to do that much, anyway."

"My early-bird students sit and wait over on those big rocks yonder. Which might at least give a bit of comfort while we work."

So I took myself off to the Printer boy and told Otis to meet me there when his lesson was finished.

This is the way Otis told about his being schooled in the fine art of conversing with a lady.

"Well, Otis, you already know how to greet a young lady, because I have seen you do so. Once the pleasantries are completed you then must ask permission to converse with her. She may not feel inclined to spend her time with you. And a lady's wishes must always be considered.

As far as topics to put forth these may take any path. If nothing occurs as a possibility consider general topics ... the weather, current happenings about Oro City, her general health, etc. The foremost conversation starters should be questions about herself. Inquiries must not be too personal to begin with or you may sound as if you're probing into her private life."

Otis remained quite self-conscious. He sat perched on a rock nearby where Isabelle sat and kept forcing his boot deeper into the rock strewn soil. He had made a groove that could have caused a passing prospector to wonder if he'd unearthed some gold.

"I see Jasper coming along now. We can meet again in a day or two and practice some make-believe conversations, if you'd like."

"That would suit me just fine, Ma'am. I am much obliged. Good bye."

And he high-tailed it over to where I now stood on the road.

For some weeks now Lucinda and Millie had felt cramped in the small room in Holiday House. One day, after the early snowfall event had come and gone, Frank White called out to them as they were returning from a walk in the woods.

"Ladies, I have a vacant room for letting if either of you be interested. The fellow who was boarding there has decided that the lengthy winter will not suit him so he left for warmer climes."

Oh, Mr. White, we've been so over-crowded in the space we've been sharing. Millie and I would most gratefully rent this second room. Millie has been joining me at the Hall for some days now, and Mr. Smithson has placed her on the payroll so it will work out perfectly!"

"Good. As soon as my young helper can finish the cleaning you are welcome to move your things in."

The following day before the two had breakfasted they carried Millie's belongings into the room across the hallway. It faced the opposite direction of Lucinda's window view, but Millie was very satisfied with it. The friends spent some time brightening the room with leftover scraps of fabric for framing the window and even began making a cheerful coverlet for the bed.

"Look. We've completely used all the fabric scraps which have been lying about. If we ever need fabric for anything at all we'll have to purchase some from Tabor's store, Lucinda.

And may I just say that these weeks with you have benefited me in so many ways? Who knows what sordid future I might have had if it were not for you and Mr. Smithson."

"Oh, Millie. I am the one who is indebted to you. You have been my guardian angel and I will forever be beholden to you! We've missed breakfast but why don't we walk down and see what might be offered for lunch."

On the way to the cook house where they took their meals they agreed to wrap the food and picnic in the hills.

The lunch offerings were meager, but they wrapped the biscuits and bacon in a clean handkerchief and hiked down to the creek. This particular spot was unpleasant and unsightly because of past placer mining so they crossed the stream by stepping on stones and managed to keep their shoes dry. Following a faint trail the two climbed up the hill to a grove of aspen that was showing-off golden fall colors and spread their shawls onto the forest floor.

"On such a day it is hard to imagine that unpleasant things occur around here." Said Lucinda. She had untied her bonnet ribbons but left it on to shade her face knowing the sun to be relentlessly intense. She did not want her skin burned nor freckled.

Millie followed her lead and then leaned back on her elbows. Tipping her head up to the sky and sighing with contentment. She didn't share her friend's concern about sun exposure. But in time she would.

Both of them heard the snapping of small branches at the very instant that a doe stepped out from the forest's concealment. All three froze. None making a move nor a sound. The deer was so near that steam could be seen wafting from her nostrils. Her huge black eyes appeared luminous and sort of liquid-like. No one dared to blink as if realizing that to do so would fracture the magical moment.

Alas! The doe blinked first and vanished back into the woods.

Once they exhaled their held breaths Millie and Lucinda shared thoughts about the unexpected visit from a wild creature.

"Do you think such an occurrence would portend a favorable effect or the opposite, Millie?"

"I've never held much store in superstitions, so for myself I will tuck the event away as a sweet secret that was awe-inspiring."

After a short time they decided to pay a visit to Augusta Tabor.

As they entered a young fellow was sweeping sawdust over the oiled wood floors. He had a goodly pile of the shavings left over and so moved the stuff to a back corner. It could be used again on the grit that got tracked in from the road. The lad's name was Caleb and he had a pronounced limp which didn't seem to interfere with restocking shelves or any other chores.

Augusta looked over at Caleb and told him to come back and finish the task in the morning. Then she turned to the ladies.

"Hello, my friends. How have you been since we were graced with that early snow?" She was perched on a stool at the counter, cyphering.

Lucinda spoke first. “We have been quite fine, Augusta. We must order woolen underwear and two blankets. And we have a spot of news.”

“Yes, indeed we do.” Millie said. “Just today I have taken a vacated room at Holiday House which is simply a most improved situation as we have been living on top of one another in Lucinda’s room.”

A shadow passed fleetingly across the store-keep’s face.

“It will be alright, Augusta, really. I am quite well and Millie will be only steps from me if she’s ever needed.”

“Of course, my dear. I have every confidence in your heartiness and you have shown such strong will-power for weeks and weeks. Please don’t mistake a passing concern of mine. I have no misgivings regarding your attempts to remain sound and fit.”

“Oh I know that it takes time to leave an abomination behind and then to expect full confidence from my friends. I have put you through so much anguish and anxiety. I owe my very life to the both of you.” She took out a handkerchief to dab at tears from around her eyes.

Heaving a sigh of relief Millie said, “Actually, along with the undergarments and blankets we’ve come to look at fabric. We’re each going to make a new gown for our performances.”

Isabelle’s face showed her surprise at this idea. It had not been discussed.

“I don’t have much on hand to choose from, but I have a catalogue behind the counter here so that you may decide on something suitable which I will order along with the needed winter items. It would only take a few weeks to arrive on a freight wagon."

Augusta climbed off the stool and bent down to get the catalogue. While she was thus occupied and Millie was handling the few remnants of material on a table, Lucinda was furtively pocketing a blue bottle of laudanum.

It had been necessary to lean over the countertop to reach the bottle. And Millie looked across at her catching her in the act.

Lucinda attempted a hurried get away, but Millie reached the door ahead of her and held out her hand for the cobalt bottle.

"No, I need this. It is my indispensable medicine. You will not snatch it away from me!" She was choking back tears and nearing a state of hysteria.

"I do not judge you nor does Augusta. We offer only love and friendship. Is this not true, Augusta?" It was necessary to wrestle the bottle from her friend.

Augusta moved toward them and drew Lucinda into a firm embrace. She held her for some long minutes until Lucinda had quieted and regained some composure. She flipped over the sign to indicate that the store was closed.

All three women sat on a bench with a notion to gather a collective mollifying of nerves.

Once calmed they each spoke of how difficult it is to remain untethered by such horrendous torments. And the fact that one must never rest on one's laurels by taking successes for granted.

"Do you think you're up to singing tonight?" Millie asked.

"Hmm, yes I believe it's the only sure way that I can gain back my equilibrium. It seems that I've been fighting the devil on his own ground for long enough."

"Augusta, it occurs to me that since you've closed the store up early you might like to accompany us for dinner and later on to the evening performance." Said Millie.

The older woman agreed to this. She would change her clothes and meet the other two at the H.H. where they would also be changing garments.

Otis had set up a time with Isabelle and was heading to the schoolhouse for his second session.

Because the weather could be stable in the fall and this day was holding warm and fine the teacher and her student met outdoors in front of the building.

Isabelle began, "Now, Otis, I'll act out the part of the young lady and you will, of course, be yourself. I'll suggest some responses as we move along. Agreed?"

"Yes, Ma'am. But what if I bungle my lines?"

"Well, then I will offer help which is the very reason we're doing this."

"You begin by greeting her properly. Let's call her 'Miss Jones'."

"Hello, Ma'am."

"Fine start, but let's agree that you have formerly been

introduced by another party. You may address her as Miss Jones."

"Hello, Miss Jones, Ma'am."

"Otis, drop the Ma'am; it's repetitious. Now you will follow by speaking some pleasantries. A few examples might be ... 'How are you today?' Or, 'Have you been enjoying this fine weather?' Or. 'How did you like the performance last evening?'

The idea is to speak of matters that are about her. People always appreciate when interest is directed toward themselves. Now you greet her and follow with some question."

Otis' sweaty face showed his nervousness and he kept pulling out his handkerchief to swipe at his neck and forehead. He was silently questioning the necessity of all this consternation. But as he was already here he determined to stick with it for a while longer.

"How are you and the weather and hello, Miss Jones?" "Humph. I tangled those words all up in a knot."

"It is okay for now. You've got the idea. Next you will need to discover topics which are of interest to her. So you must do a bit of preliminary snooping. Maybe you've seen her gathering flowers. Maybe you know how she makes her living here in the Gulch. Keep your statements general. Avoid being too personal."

"So let's give it a try. You say 'Hello' and she says 'Hello'. Now it's back to you."

"How are you doing these days?"

"I have been quite well, thank you."

"I heard you sing in Smithson's Hall with Miss Poole."

"Oh? Did you, indeed?"

"Yes, I did, indeed I did."

"Now what, Miss L.? I forget what's next."

"I believe you're getting the idea. Just remember not to be overly repetitive. If you'd like one more session I could meet with you tomorrow at this same time and place."

"Alright by me. I sure do appreciate you taking the time to school me."

While walking down the road to meet Jasper at Doc's he tried to keep from running the lesson over and over in his mind. He told himself that it had been hard enough the first time. No need adding to his torment and torture.

Otis met with Isabelle the following day for less than an hour.

"Now, Otis, yesterday you brought forth the fact that the fictitious Miss Jones performs as a singer. So why don't you keep that topic alive for a bit? You might say, 'How long have you been singing?' 'Did you have formal training?' 'Do you enjoy performing with Miss Poole?'

"Miss Jones will give you answers which you will then be able to build a conversation on. The more you practice the better you will become. This is the way it is with all things. At first you may think that this method seems contrived but in time the conversing will feel more relaxed and natural. I hope you will have much success in beginning a new friendship with the 'Miss Jones', Otis."

"I'm not feeling confident at this time, Miss Isabelle, but even so I intend to take a goodly attempt at it very soon. Why maybe even tonight. I thank you most sincerely. Good day."

"Good day to you. Maybe you will come by on a future day and tell me how you fared."

"Yes. I will."

Isabelle mused silently that her adult student was a quick study.

Later on when I met up with Otis we took some time to tie up any loose ends concerning young ladies.

"So now tell me, Otis, did the school mistress present you with a certificate of achievement to carry under your hat from here on out?"

"No. Was I supposed to get such a paper? Because she didn't give me nothing like this."

"No, ho! There exists no such a thing. I'm just joshing at your expense."

"Shouldn't treat a friend so mean, Jasper. You know how much suffering I've been going through with all this proper back and forth talk with Miss Millie. I could use a dose of encouragement from you."

"Uh huh."

We were almost to Doc's but turned in to the nearby saloon for a whiskey since we completely missed lunch.

"I see what you're getting at, Otis. What say we go along to Pepper's stall now and quietly do some practicing before the evening's performance begins? That way you will have all the fancy words on the tip of your tongue ready to use when you need them?"

This idea gave some comfort to Otis as we came abreast of Pepper's lean-to.

"You ol' bandit, Pepper. Looks like you've got yourself some company this night. You got a name, mule?"

"Look here, Jasper. Some scoundrel has been dipping into Pepper's grain bag. Not once but a few times at least. Nasty business to steal from a dumb animal. Beg pardon, Pepper."

"Huh. Now you mention it, the bag is more than half empty and we just topped it off yesterday. Guess I'll put the word out along the Gulch road that a petty thief is here and about.

You keep a watch out, Pepper. Don't be giving your feed away or you'll be on meager rations. And it's well known all along the Gulch that you're a mite greedy about your grain."

"Let's try a back and forth for a short time, Jasper. I'm keen to move some practiced words from the back of my throat to the surface of my lips."

"So I'll be Miss Millie and you only have to be your lumbering self."

"Try to help my self-esteem if you are able, Jasper. This is hard enough for me, and you know it too. I'll start."

"Hello, Miss Millie. How are you enjoying this soft evening air?"

"That's real good, Otis. Mighty fine in fact."

"Could we just stick to our plan for a quick minute?" Otis said frowning and he began again.

"I am fond of this time of the year here in the Gulch." This was my line.

"I sure do enjoy your performances. You are a fine singer of songs."

"Well, now, Otis, that was real good. But leave off the songs part."

"I did know my mistake as soon as it was out of my mouth. If I slow down and think I know I won't be doing so much of the repeating. Miss Isabelle pointed this out to me so I reckon it's something I need to work on."

"You ask me, I'd say you're ready to say some fine words to Miss Millie."

"Well then what say we clean up and work our way down to the Hall for some soft entertainment?"

"No time for a meal? That's somewhat extreme. We already missed the mid-day meal. Imagine if our empty stomachs start chorusing along with the music?"

Otis stopped on the road to consider this possibility. Then he said, "That would be embarrassing for certain. Okay, let's go on ahead and eat our supper and skip over the cleaning up for today."

The evenings were getting colder so we wasted little time getting down to Doc's. Once inside we spotted Doc shadowed by Buster, just walking out of the back kitchen room.

"Evening, Gentlemen. A little on the early side for supper, but it won't be more than twenty minutes or so."

"Well, a quick whiskey then. Join us Doc?" I said.

"Sounds good to me. Be back shortly, Buster. Sweep up some while you're standing around waiting to serve."

Buster grunted and went to seek out a broom.

Before entering the saloon I knocked my hat against my leg to rid it of dust. This never did much good, but I sort of did it without thinking.

"Can't see why you do that thing with your hat, Jasper. It looks the same before and after."

"Just a habit, Otis."

The three of us sidled up to the bar and each asked for whiskey.

"Say, Doc, you called us gentlemen when you greeted us just now. Do you think that's a fair description of us or just a slip of the tongue?

"You see Otis is hoping to change from bum to dandy so's his sweetheart will treat him more tenderly, Doc."

"Didn't mean much by calling you gentlemen. Just figure you more along those lines than most of these ill-mannered miners here about."

"Makes sense, I guess. Speaking of unruly miners Otis and me just noted a thief's doings up at Pepper's lean-to. Someone with quick hands and sneaky ways has been dipping into my burro's grain bag. Pepper won't raise an alarm. He's so contrary that he'd probably give the thief an encouraging nudge towards the bag." I turned my head towards Doc and then asked, "Got any ideas of who owns a mule and tethers it with Pepper?"

"Let me chew on it for a while. If I come up with a name or two I'll let you know first chance."

We ate our supper unhurriedly and then walked on down to Smithson's. It was right chilly inside the hall but got warmer as the place filled up with enthusiastic men.

We were both satisfied with the bench seats good and near the piano which Lucinda saved for us, good to her promise.

Piano music and songs filled the roadway and outdoor atmosphere with such mirth and joie de vivre… that caused people passing by to be filled with longing for a gentle more civilized town. Those lucky enough to be inside felt encased in a soft honeyed space.

Once the show began Otis and me were entranced not only by the musical program but by the loveliness of the performers. Neither of us could quite drag our eyes from the ladies. Not even for a moment.

When the final number was finished the two of us with stars in our eyes were swept out of the building on a human tide of miners. Only we chose not to follow the human current into the saloons as we were very much determined to have some congenial words with Lucinda and Millie.

After helping Smithton to sweep up and restore order to the room they wrapped on shawls and went out into the road, where they were met by me and Otis.

"Sure was a fine show, Miss Lucinda. I enjoyed every single song and truly could just sit and listen to you all night."

"Why that's flattering, Jasper. I believe I should scratch around these parts so that I might find a few new songs to add to the program. Some of the men have become regular attendees – they likely have the lyrics to some of the numbers memorized by now."

We two chatted amicably as we walked up the road arms not quite touching but our heads tipped toward each other in order to hear ourselves over the raucous din coming from numerous saloons.

Several paces behind us the second couple was experiencing awkward pauses after each exchange. Otis was struggling mightily and Millie was trying her utmost to put him at ease. He had run through every rehearsed comment without hardly pausing to allow Millie a response.

"You have a nice singing voice."

"Why thank ..."

"You must've had lots of training to be so good."

"Actually no. In fact ..."

"How do you like living in such a rough place? And how come you came up here to the Gulch, anyways?"

Finally Millie took matters into her own hands.

"Tell me, Mr. Walls, a little about yourself. How long have you been here in Oro City?"

"Well, let me think on it for a minute. Um, just about two years all tallied up. I was hauling a freight wagon up Mosquito Pass early last spring when I met up with Jasper over by American Flats. We partnered up soon as we crossed over the summit. For one reason or the other since then we have done most everything together so I guess we've stuck with it through thick and thin."

Just up ahead Lucinda and me stopped in front of H.H. as we'd decided to wait for Otis and Millie to draw near.

We four exchanged pleasant goodbyes and Lucinda and Millie went inside.

Once back at Doc's Otis and me, though pretty near tuckered out from the evening doings, stopped short in front of our enclave. A rank odor assaulted us. Some loudly snoring fellow was stretched out on the pallets that we'd been using for several months.

"What's this then?" Said Otis.

Us friends tried to make sense of the situation.

"Don't think it would do to wake the man from a sound sleep. He may come to much like a disturbed bear, a' growling and a' swinging. What say we find Doc so that he can straighten out the mess?" I said using a quiet voice.

Doc was not soft-hearted regarding shirkers. In fact he had two burly, wooly men with him who stood back while Doc had a word with the sleepy fellow.

"Who are you? You pay for a sleeping place before it's yours for the night. Way it works in the Gulch."

The guy became belligerent using foul words and snarls, so the two muscle-men held him arms and legs. The situation went from bad to worse with wrestling, gouging, and shouting. Before long, though, the man was on his back being held down by four others.

Right away Doc sent Buster, none too pleased to be awakened from his slumber, down the road almost as far along as Tom Starr's house to alert a committeeman that a jail space would be needed presently.

And so, with plenty of commotion the trouble-maker, bound hands and feet, was hauled to the lock-up to await a hearing/ trial first thing the next day.

Before tucking in we gave our straw pallets a good shaking, but it didn't do much to rid the space of a lingering stench.

The next morning was quite cold, a blue sky belying the below-freezing temperatures. It actually felt like deep winter, although there was no snow on the ground nor in the thin clouds. The western peaks were dark grey and not covered in new snow.

Lucinda had spent an uneasy night. She was bothered by a moderate craving for a dose of her medicine. She felt annoyed that her people kept the cobalt bottle just beyond her reach. On the one hand she was less tormented than before by the addiction, but on the other hand at times she immediately wanted what she told herself she needed.

In spite of her testy mood she greeted Millie with a smile.

"Hello, my dear. I think I need to go back for a second shawl. You look bundled up, though."

"Yes Lucinda, I have a coat on under this shawl. I'll be waiting right here, but hurry please."

As the two friends walked along swiftly to breakfast they decided not to waste breath talking. It was just too miserably cold.

They walked into the cookhouse where they took meals and found the place overly heated by a large stove.

"Oh my goodness, it is one extreme or another. It's stuffy hot in here. Let's take off some of these outer garments, Millie. Here, there's a spot next to me where we can pile them."

Their faces had been reddened from the outdoors but presently showed a sheen of sweat beads. A wet wool smell permeated throughout the room.

They were served corn fritters today. A novelty for sure. And the coffee was strong and hot.

"Well, do tell me what you think of Jasper, Lucinda. He seems an affable fellow."

"Oh. I don't have a strong opinion of him one way or the other. I imagine that we're compatible enough. Conversing with him is not a strain. I guess I just don't feel any kind of special attraction." And she thought to herself, "I'd like him a whole lot more if he could be a resolute supplier of my medicine."

Millie studied her friend and told herself, "In the dream or in the waking world Lucinda is in torment again. Maybe a dose of the laudanum would not be so much of a stumbling block to her recovery." She resolved to confer with Augusta soon.

Later in the day when she knew Lucinda to be resting Millie hurried into Tabor's store. When she entered she noticed two of Red Stocking's hens shopping along the far wall, so she ducked her head behind a display of mining tools, shovels and assorted implements. The painted ladies paid for some foodstuffs and left.

Millie sighed with relief that she wasn't made to greet them in any way.

"You have never been part of that way of life, Millie. Why do you imagine that one of those gals would show you any recognition?"

"I did lodge in that shady quarter for a few days, remember? Before you rescued me?"

"Of course I remember. But if I recall during that short time you had little if no contact with the working girls. Am I right, or do you recall the situation differently?"

"Oh, Augusta, you are correct. I saw nothing of the sporting women's comings and goings. But I did have a lengthy interview with the Madam of the house. She may have pointed me out to some of them. I know it's unlikely but I do have some moments of anxiety when I am in close proximity with any of them."

"Well, my dear, you worry over much. Now did you need to shop for something or another? Or are you simply paying me a visit?"

"I do not need a thing. But my mind is troubled. It's our

Lucinda, you see. She has been exhibiting behaviors that bring to mind her anguished torment during that time not too far in the past. Her addiction to what she refers to as her medicine."

"Well, I do feel that Lucinda has made admirable progress, Millie. I'm no expert but I've seen a few others as they suffer from the same malady. It would be no hindrance to her recovery if she were to have a small portion, say a spoonful, of her remedy now and again."

"Augusta, I was thinking this very same thing! I would cautiously submit that in offering her such a modest dose she might feel her outgoing exuberance once more."

"Here is an open bottle of the substance. Take it with you now and when you have poured out the portion and served it to her you may then bring the bottle back here. We will hold it in reserve for these particularly strained bouts that our dear friend suffers."

"Oh you are a godsend, Augusta. You have come to my aid multiple times. I wish that I could repay you even if in a trifling way."

The pleasant lady brushed this remark away in her characteristically benevolent manner.

Me and Otis hustled over to Pepper's lean-to at an early hour the following day, first stopping at Tabor's store for a bag of feed. The burro's breathing was causing clouds of mist to halo his head.

"Ho, look at you with an angel wreath circling your muzzle.

Everyone here about knows it must belong to the beast standing next to you. Your habits testify that it don't fit you." I said.

Otis was pouring the newly purchased grain into the feed-bag when he looked over and noticed that the mule tied next to Pepper didn't look none too healthy. Matted fur and ribs sticking out indicated a sure sign of neglect. On closer inspection he noted that one ear had been chewed on, so was now only part of an ear.

"What do you make of this animal's plight, Jasper?"

"Don't rightly know, but I think I'll look into this saddle pannier, see if we'll come across some clues."

I lifted the bag from the saddle horn and laid it on the ground. Both of us made a careful search of the contents but when we finished looking the find consisted of refuse and useless worn tack and rope. Finally we offered the feedbag to the mule and watered him as well.

"What say we go on down to Tom Starr's and get some of his remedies for mending horses and such? While working on his placers Sam and me noticed his knowhow in treating all variety of animal ailment."

Approaching the man's outbuildings we found Starr busy at organizing tools, pans, and boards which were used on the placers.

"What ya' doing here, Tom?"

"Hi ya' Otis, Jasper. I'm a' storing this mess for use next spring. Winter's chasing summer faster 'n' all get-out."

"Say, Tom, we've got a mule up to Pepper's lean-to looks

pretty beat up. We're wondering would you take time out to hike on up there with us, see what there might be done to help the animal to mend"?

"Sure thing, Otis. Don't mind leaving these tiresome chores for a spell. Could go along right now and have a look-see if that suits."

Once back up the road us men ducked into the stable. Tom gave the mule a good looking-over, but became more irritated by the minute.

"Who owns this animal, do you know"?

We both shook our heads 'no'.

And then I said, "We pawed through that panier but came up with no clues. There's a ne'er-do-well cooling his heels in the jail tent. He was using our space at Doc's last night and got riled up when asked to move along. Mining commission hauled him away cussing and thrashing about. Might could be his. Just a guess, though."

"Appears to be mighty neglected and beat up by a wild cat maybe." Said Otis.

"Tell ya' what I'm thinking to do. I'll take this fellow on down to my place and fix him a place in the barn. Then I'll go on over to the jail and see if that scoundrel will fess up about ownership. I'll let you know what comes of it. You don't want the real owner to come along fussing about his missing property if it's the wrong guy."

"That's mighty fine of you, Tom. Thanks for rescuing the animal and getting us out of a fix in the bargain." I said.

"Can't abide seeing a dumb beast mistreated. One thing I just won't tolerate, boys."

Tom tied a rope to the mule and started off leading it down the Gulch road.

Before he got too far away Otis called out, "Say, why don't you come into Doc's at suppertime and we'll treat you to a meal and a whiskey?"

"Okay. I'll take you up on that kind offer. Could always use some friendly conversation along with a toot. See you both around sundown, then."

After Tom was gone I took time for some parting words with Pepper.

"Seems like to me you could've been more helpful. I'm a' thinking to take you along to Isabelle Laughlin. See if she'd be willing to school you in the English language. That way you'd be a sight more useful with puzzlements such as this one. 'Stead of you just standing around idle."

Pepper showed mild disdain and shook his head vigorously. And for good measure tried to get his teeth on my arm.

"None of your impertinence, you troublesome burro."

Saying this last bit to Pepper brought to mind how many people have helped me with English along the way.

I thought to myself, "I've learned some fancy new words while listening to Lucinda and I try them out whenever I can. Speaking English has always been a source of pride ever since arriving in this new land. I sometimes dream in German but I haven't slipped back into speaking my mother tongue a single time that I can recall."

Earlier we had a notion to get shaves and baths and even get our clothes washed, so that's where we are headed.

As we ambled along Otis said, "One of these times we need to parlay about when to go back to the cabin."

"I've been enjoying Lucinda's performances so much and even more so now that we have managed to walk the ladies home afterwards. I got to admit, Otis, I haven't given much thought as to when to return to the cabin."

"I see what you're getting at. If we were to leave Oro now we'd be taking the chance of some other fellows jumping our claims. Our girls, I mean to say."

"Uh huh. So this is what I put to you. Let's hold off going back and let the first couple of snows determine when to go."

"Okay by me, Jasper. I mean to get to know Millie a whole lot better."

Meanwhile Millie approached Lucinda with her usual bravado. She had to appear empathetic while at the same time standing her ground. She rapped on her friend's door.

After a longer than necessary wait time she opened up to Millie. And she looked as if she'd been dragged through a knothole.

"May I come in, Lucinda? I have here a small draft of your medicine. I'm just supposing that a dose will perk you up."

Then she brushed past her friend and walked towards the window, her back to the room. Taking the spoon in one hand she poured the syrup carefully and then handed it to Lucinda.

Lucinda licked the spoon clean and ran her tongue along her lips over and over again. As yet she had not spoken a single word.

But presently she said, "I do thank you, Millie. I guess I should offer my thanks to Augusta, as well."

"There's time for all that when you feel more yourself. For now, why don't you attend to your toilette? And in the meantime I'll freshen up in my room and meet you outside."

But before she did anything she hustled over to the store and handed off the blue bottle to Augusta.

Once again outside Millie said, "Just listen to the wind wailing through the trees."

Lucinda nodded, "Most assuredly snow will be making a presence in Oro City before morning. Maybe even before we're abed tonight."

Wrapping her shawl more securely around her shoulders, Millie asked, "Do you suppose the storms here in the Gulch will be as wretched as those we had to endure on the plains?"

"Never having lived through a winter here I can't predict how merciless nor ferocious the winter storms will be. I cannot even offer a conjecture on the subject. We at least have decent shelter and situations with pay, so is that not a vast improvement over the wagon trains, hmm?

"Also, I am grateful that Frank White has opened up some

air passages to our rooms so that we will have some heat from the downstairs stove."

Before that evening's performance Lucinda and Millie agreed to rehearse the words to a song neither of them knew very well. "Beautiful Dreamer".

"Millie, we'll sing the chorus and first lines together and then I'll sing the next few alone.

"So, 'Beautiful dreamer wake unto me; starlight and dewdrops are waiting for thee - then you join in with 'Beautiful dreamer queen of my song, list while I woo thee with sweet melody; gone are the cares of life's busy throng.'

And we finish together, 'Beautiful dreamer wake unto me.'"

"I think this will sound splendid, Lucinda."

And the two rehearsed until both were satisfied.

The following day Otis was rewashing yet another placer claim. When quite suddenly the quietude was split by loud, foul hollering which was issuing forth from the road above the creek. The noise was so deafening that it brought several miners running from all directions.

Otis stood back watching those who were lurching and gouging, kicking and stomping one another. There was so much fierce activity that it was difficult to see just how many were involved in the melee.

As the pugilists' wrestling began to slow it was possible to see that actually just a couple of men were involved. The two had bleeding faces and were covered with muck from the dirty snow. Their clothes were in tatters, whether from this fight or from ordinary wear and tear.

"Nothin' but chippies in that gooseberry ranch. That whore stuck me twice with my own knife, I tell you."

"She told Red Stockings that you were trying to sneak out before her money was paid! She said you were a cheat and a rogue."

"That harlot poured so much whiskey into me I could hardly stand. By the time I was able to see straight there she was a' helping herself to my stash of dust 'twas inside my boot. She herself is the lowest kind of thief."

All these assertions of fury were spat out from the mouths of the fighters.

Once the reason for the fight was out in the open the two were separated and held to the ground.

"I say we send for a commissioner to investigate the truth of all this." Said one of the bystanders.

And from another, "'Fore the commission gets here let's go get the hellcat."

Grunts of consent were issued from the crowd.

The commission interviewed all the involved parties and also a few additional miners who testified that the wench in question was indeed capable of aberrant behaviors. It was agreed that her near-murderous attack with the knife sealed her fate.

The sentence was pronounced. The woman would be hung

that very day.

Almost every person who lived in Oro City and the surrounds wanted to see this hanging. It therefore turned into quite a spectacle, as 'Hatchet Nose Callie' would be the first female to swing from a rope in California Gulch.

"Did you happen to see any of the day's spectacle, Otis?' I said as we were meeting for supper at Doc's.

"Sure did, Jasper. Hardly a soul in Lower Oro could avoid the doings - the noise carried from here to the Arkansas. I wanted to stay with my work but I got washed along as the tide crowded as near to the ferocious show as possible."

"Scuttlebutt is there's a' hanging late this evening. You thinking of going?"

"Not me. I don't care to see such events ordinarily. And I shudder to be watching a female swingin'. Was you thinking you'd like to go on down and witness?"

"No, not me, either. I believe I feel the same as you."

We talked about 'Hatchet Nose Callie' with Doc who for once took time to sit with us, as we spooned leftover venison stew onto our plates and drank mugs of beer.

"I hear tell she's only been in the Gulch a month. Seems Callie came up from Denver City in a rush since for some weeks the local authorities had been dealing with complaints about her and some other whores who'd been living in a rundown tent. Even then she was just a scant hour away from being jailed." Said Doc.

"Ever hear a tale of how she come by that name?" I asked.

"Couple of miners standing nearby as the fight ensued were telling this here version." Said Otis. "Seems on the way west Callie's wagon train had a run-in with a large band of Indians... in the midst of the encounter a young brave wielding a hatchet fell slain at Callie's feet.

"Story goes that as she grabbed hold of the Indian's hatchet, somehow she got throwed against the wagon wheel. Her nose was bent all out of whack. But she still had hold of that hatchet.``

"Can't help feeling sorry for Callie. It's a tough enough life for men with skills and strength." I said to my friends. "For the gentler sex it is twice as difficult to get a toe-hold once they leave family and farm behind. I'm awful glad Lucinda and Millie have found a way to get by with their music."

We said our goodbyes to our friends and headed out. A biting wind was predictably coming in from the northwest and nearly snatched our breath away.

We noticed the new saloon in final stages of completion that was rumored to include a fancier type space for sitting and conversing. A place in which a respectable lady could enjoy being with a gentleman suitor. It would be a level up in civility for Oro City. "The Gilded Lily Tea Room"

On our way to Smithson's Hall for the evening's performance Otis and me walked unhurriedly past this new place in spite of the bitter wind creeping under our coat sleeves and collars.

"Say, Jasper, won't this establishment be a fine place to take the ladies?"

"Indeed it would, my friend."

The last musical number "Beautiful Dreamer" concluded the entertainment.

Otis and me waited right by the door inside the Hall for the ladies. It was too cold to stand about outside freezing.

"Take care to wrap up warm and tight, Millie. Lucinda. That wind could freeze a hot-blooded person solid even if he's a' running flat out. If he's not smothered in layers head to toe that is." Said Otis.

The four of us hurried up the road to Holiday House. No one bothered with useless chatter as the wind blew our words off into the surrounding forests and beyond.

It was comfort enough to lean in close to one another so as to afford some shelter. For the present, words could wait.

Once we arrived at H.H. we were greeted by Frank White who bid us come into his quarters so that we could thaw out next to the stove. We did not hesitate to accept his offer.

With reddened hands and a dripping nose I felt myself slowly warming up.

"Mr. White, have you met our friends, Jasper Gratz and Otis Walls?"

"No, Miss Lucinda. I haven't had the pleasure. How do, fellows?"

After introductions were made the ladies took their leave.

Frank then asked about both Otis' and my own occupations which were not much different than any others in the Gulch, of course.

"And what about yourself, Frank, is it? Do you use a day in its entirety managing this here boarding house?" I asked.

"This is what I was doing and only this, until a short time ago. Sort of thought myself a shirker. Now it happens that I am to be involved with the new saloon which will have an additional space for genteel folks to sit and converse 'thout being buggered by the rowdies."

"Sounds like you've nailed it with that idea, Frank. Must have been an expense though." Said Otis as he readied himself for the frigid outdoors.

"Funny that you say that. As it happens I found a nugget hiding in a sort of eddy right here in the creek. Don't know how so many fellows could have overlooked it after so many years of working these claims. But I just said to myself that I'd like to use my windfall to do somethin' special that ladies would get enjoyment from."

Back at Doc's me and Otis fell onto our pallets and called it a day.

The following day after a breakfast I could easily have foregone, as it was leftover stew from the night before and not so appetizing the first go 'round. I took myself a walk over to Pepper's stall.

As I approached my burro emitted a sort of friendly whinny.

"Well ain't that nice. So maybe you missed me and not too proud to say?"

Wrong thing to think that he had changed his manner overnight.

He started up by pawing the dirt and sudden-like kicked up his hind legs 'til he was bucking and braying at the top of his lungs. His screeching was so loud he could probably be heard all the way down to Tom Starr's.

I was completely caught off guard by the suddenness of his change. But thankfully I was out of his range of action so I just stood back and watched in stupefaction.

"You have the temperament of a grizzly-wildcat mix. No wonder you don't have no friends. If you don't settle yourself down real quick I will not be taking you for a ramble around the Gulch as was my earlier plan."

Lots of snorting and blowing through his nose followed. I came cautiously around to his head in order to throw the rope on but he tucked his entire head into a corner of the shed and shook off all efforts on my part to halter him.

At this point I'd had about enough of his aggravation. So I turned on my heel to leave. But as was his way Pepper gave my arm a gentle nudge and curled his lip. That mocking look as if to say "Sorry, slacker." Understandable attitude since as of late I had paid very little attention to him.

As I loped along with the burro on his lead his demeanor was mollified. Anyone looking would think him a well-disciplined, hard-working paragon of his breed.

"Ha!"

After all this I determined to use the remainder of the day 'smithing up at the Printer Boy forge. I was fairly certain that plenty of bit sharpening was needed.

"Hey, Jasper. Where you been? There's a week's worth of sharpening awaiting you."

"Hi ya. Cal. I figured some work would be needed doing. I'll get my apron and build up the fire right away."

"While you're at it I'll hang around and swap some newsy stories if you've a mind to."

"That will suit me just fine. I got some hearsay about the new saloon on down the road a piece. A fellow name of Frank White came across a lucky find awhile back. His story goes along these lines. Minute while I lift this anvil into place."

I was working up a sweat only after a few minutes. It felt good, though.

"Anyway ol' Frank found a good-sized nugget in the creek back behind his boarding house. So he's bought into the newest saloon and has had an extension tacked on to one side. Get this. Plans to make it a fancy tea room for the genteel folks."

"Well that ought to fill up one table. Ain't too many with that classiness around in all of Oro City. Prob'ly not even in the entire of the upper Arkansas region. Can't see too much success in doing such a thing. Can you?"

"Don't exactly know one way or t'other but I do hope he has luck with the idea. It is a bold one."

Cal took his leave to ride a man-trip down into the mine so as to give direction to one of the crews. The mine had been working a stamp mill for some time and the gold from the crushed ore was making a handsome profit.

I thought about all this while watching my friend climb into the steel car hooked onto cables that would carry him down into the bowels of the mine. I wondered if this type of work might suit Otis. I'd have to remember to ask him first thing.

The day was making me feel productive and useful in my own way. I had a growing need to accomplish a suitable career so that my future would hold some appeal to Lucinda if she would allow me to court her proper-like. I sure couldn't keep my thoughts from shifting into her territory. She held me enthralled.

That she had had trouble I felt certain. But the nature of the trouble had me baffled. I held back in delving into this personal area. I sure wouldn't like to intrude where I was not welcome. This knowing would be in our future - not in our present.

My German mother would say, "Don't go digging deep. You might get buried." Or something along those lines.

Which reminds me now that I have not sent off a letter to my family in Aachen for months. I will write to them today when I finish my work here.

I stopped in at Tabor's store to purchase some paper and a stamp. Mrs. T. was not behind the counter. Instead her husband Horace was waiting on customers. I stepped up and introduced myself.

"Howdy, Mr. Tabor. Name's Jasper Gratz. I do smithy work up at the Printer Boy."

"I'm Horace or H.A.W. as some call me. My wife, Augusta, has been minding our store here for over a year. I've been up to Buckskin Joe prospecting, but with scant success. I'm only here for a week - need to get back to my claims. Can't leave them untended. Too many jumpers."

"Everyone in Oro City thinks Augusta is top notch. She's always the first to give sound advice and also the one to offer assistance to those in need. You have a fine wife, Horace. By the way what's all them initials stand for?"

"Horace Austin Warner. And that's a right fine compliment for my wife, so I'll be pleased to pass it along to her. She's mending my britches and shirts upstairs. What can I do you for?"

"Just need some writing paper and a stamp. I'll be sending an update to my family and hope to get it posted before the mail goes out at the end of the week."

I'll be honest and say most miners carried a rankness due to a lack of bathing, but Tabor's fumes were permeating the room in vast measure. 'Account of the stink I bore a hastiness to transact my business and be gone.

On my walk to meet Otis I tarried in Pepper's stall seeing after his needs. That is mainly checking on his supplies.

"Well, burro. Are you going to welcome me or be inhospitable? Makes little difference one way or t'other."

He gave me one of his insolent looks and his ear twitched forward. Before anything else I checked his water bucket and then carried it down to the creek to refill. Next after seeing that his grain bag was three quarters full I petted his head and gave him a rub down with an old piece of blanket. As I turned to go, he blew out a halfhearted snort as a parting shot.

"Always has to have the last word." I muttered to no one in particular.

Thinking about my own hygiene I turned into the bathhouse

and bought a tub soak.

Feeling refreshed, from there I took a notion to check on the progress of the so-called "Tea Room".

Workers were busy and I spotted Frank White arranging some muslin cloths on the table tops. The place had only five tables but the room held a particular look of stylishness and tastefulness. Somehow it didn't matter that it lacked scale and grandeur. This tweren't St. Louis after all.

"So when's the opening to be, Frank? Looks like could be any day now."

"You're right, Jasper. As a matter of fact, grand opening is tomorrow evening. You should come and bring Otis. Lucinda and Millie have already said to expect them here directly after the show at Smithson's."

"Well then Otis and me will show up and hopefully be escorting them."

Millie was still giving Lucinda a spoonful of laudanum, kinda stretching the doses over a day and a half to two or so and Lucinda had been showing some satisfactory progress. But with such vile addictions a person couldn't look too far down the road without expecting to be tripped up and tumbling backwards now and again.

"This weather is turning cold and snowy quicker than I anticipated, Millie."

"Yes. I'm not especially fond of frigid wind like we had the other night."

"Let's go across and see if our order has come on a freight in the last couple days."

"Splendid idea, Millie."

"Augusta, how are you today? You look a bit rested what with your Mr. being here to help out for a few days."

"Yes, Lucinda, I have been able to catch up on some personal matters that had been gathering cobwebs. Nice to see the two of you. And look at what came in on yesterday's freight! It's all boxed up yet, but let's see how much of the order actually came."

Within the sizable box the three ladies unpacked two woolen blankets, two sets of long underwear and warm, sturdy tall boots with laces rather than buttons.

"Oh my! And just in the nick of time as it seems that winter is fast approaching. We very nearly froze walking from the Hall with Jasper and Otis the other night." Millie said.

As the items were placed on the counter so that prices could be tabulated in the store ledger Augusta said, "Now I have two woolen scarves here under the shelf. One for each of you. The idea is to tie the scarf over a bonnet to keep wind and snow off your head and your ears warm."

Lucinda tied a colorful scarf over her straw bonnet and looked at her reflection in a mirror that Augusta held in front of her face.

"Well, I guess the idea is warmth and not fashion. It looks quite frumpy. But I am grateful for your thoughtfulness, Augusta. And I speak for Millie and myself. "

"Absolutely. As for myself I know that every time I step out into the cold I'll be thinking what a thoughtful friend we have." Said Millie.

They went back to their rooms to drop off the items but brought the scarves along to dinner at the cookhouse. Presently the weather was holding calm but later as they'd be leaving the Hall it could well be a different story.

Just as they left the H.H. a riderless horse came streaking up the Gulch road from somewhere down below.

"That is a dangerous hazard in this locale! I can't imagine why a man would allow his animal to run wild." Said Lucinda.

"It's likely a runaway I would think. Let's inquire from that group of miners yonder."

"Good evening. Might any of you know to whom that galloping horse belongs? Such doings make the road a perilous place for walking." Lucinda said to the trio.

"Aren't you the singers at Smithson's Hall?"

"Yes. You are quite correct. We do perform most evenings. But what of the errant horse? The owner?" Asked Millie again.

"None of us recognized the horse as one from around these parts. We might just go along now and see what's what." He doffed his hat as did the other two and hurried away.

"Hmm. Well, Lucinda. Might hear the story later at the Hall. Right now I'm wanting something hot for supper. And you?"

As the two friends sat at table for the evening's repast, which was typical - beans, cornbread, and beer - they spoke of the riderless horse.

A passing miner with well-worn bitches and a heavy grey beard stopped by their table and offered an opinion.

"That horse was roped and brought to the commission building just now. There's talk of it appearing to be the one an outlaw was riding down by the Cache Creek placers a day or two ago. Seems he was attempting to jump a claim when some men chased him out of that camp and into the area of Iowa Gulch."

"Oh. Where is Iowa Gulch from here in Oro City?" Asked Lucinda, attempting to sound only moderately interested. She didn't like to encourage idle conversation with strangers.

"Why it's just the next gulch to the south of this one. Sorry to in'erupt your meal. Hope you are entertaining tonight at Smithson's."

"Yes. We will be there later you may be assured." Said Millie.

After the fellow left Millie said, "It seems that there are so many scoundrels in these parts. I wonder if the horse belongs to such a fugitive as that miner described."

The next day in spite of the weather being quite frigid, folks up and down the Gulch were stopping to speculate on what might have happened to the Cache Creek desperado.

By afternoon, however, there was an answer. A body was found on the banks of the Arkansas between Oro and Granite frozen to a stiffness.

And after searching the dead man's belongings a

commissioner displayed the findings for all to see. Three thumb-nail-sized gold nuggets, a wanted poster folded several times and three pistols fastened to a bandoleer and finally a knife strapped to one leg.

The wanted poster said: 'WANTED FOR MURDER - HOLDUPS - ROBBERIES Reward - dead or alive!!

And a crude drawing of the man's face was on the bottom half of the sheet.

"Why he's the last member of the Espinoza gang!" Said a work-worn miner standing close by.

"I'm going to take these weapons and nuggets with me down to the committee. I plan to propose an auction so's any person can bid on the firearms and knives.

"I aim to propose that the gold be used to build a sturdy jailhouse. All are welcome to a meeting tomorrow at Tom Starr's and we'll make the decision as a community.

"Gather together mid-afternoon. Get the word out, folks. I'll ask for help in hauling this blackguard's remains down the road. "

Several miners volunteered for the duty.

The snow fell in the Gulch that same day from late afternoon through the night and was still coming down in the morning.

Upon awakening Millie peered out her window and gasped. The snow covered the entire landscape. She dressed in the warm long underwear and pulled on a second dress over the first.

Then she went across the hall and knocked on her friend's door.

Lucinda responded immediately to the knock.

"Good morning, Millie. Have you looked out your window, yet?"

"Yes. I did and then dressed in every garment that I own. Look. Two gowns. And my heavy shawl."

"Well. The snow sure looks beautiful, doesn't it? But look at your shoes. Let's lace up our new boots and tie scarves over our bonnets. Then we can walk down to breakfast."

Upon going through the H.H. door the ladies found it was not an easy matter of moving through the snow. They each stepped down into two feet of fresh-fallen snow.

The wind was not blowing and the world was silent. But the snow was falling so fast that even finding the road was a challenge.

"Maybe we should forgo breakfast and wait until the snow lets up. We may get in trouble trying to walk through these depths."

"Let's try for a while longer, Lucinda. Why don't you walk where I put my feet down? When I tire we'll change places."

And so moving along through snow that reached to the tops of their knee-high boots while holding their skirts up high they managed to reach the cookhouse in due time.

They stepped into a well-heated room. Only six others had managed to come in for breakfast. They were all talking about the ongoing snowfall.

"This ain't nothin'. Just an early reminder that if you were thinking of getting you'd better git now or stay till the spring thaws."

The scraggly-faced man in miners' garb called this back into the room as he went out into the snowy world.

The cook had managed flapjacks with molasses and hot bitter coffee.

"What should we do with our morning, Millie? Maybe go over to the Hall and rehearse our musical selections?"

"That would be a sound proposal. I'm forever needing to improve on my vocals so that I may remain worthy of being your harmonist. Without a doubt it is your sweet voice which draws the crowds. And I strive to complement your talent in any way that I am able."

"Oh you flatter me overmuch. You are equally popular with our audiences, Millie. But I do agree that rehearsing is never a waste of time. Although I'm finding myself wondering whether we'll have much of a crowd tonight considering the amount of snowfall."

The two ladies took considerable time redressing in their outer garments and then went out into the snow once more.

They hadn't gone but a few yards when Lucinda heard her name being called and stopped to see who it was out in the white world.

"Lucinda. I'm surprised to see you outside in weather like this. Hello, Millie."

"Hello, Jasper. It is really not so much of an inconvenience if one is properly dressed. And we have all the warmth we need. Do we not, Millie?"

"Indeed we do. High-top boots just like any of the men wear. And so on."

"We were just on our way to Smithson's Hall to rehearse for a few hours. Although tonight we may not have much of an audience with all this snow." Said Lucinda.

"No. A crowd is quite unlikely. I would wager that a goodly number of placer miners will be moving along to warmer climes just as soon as transport can be arranged. A dozen jumped on the stage to Denver City yesterday afternoon."

"My goodness. Well what about you and Otis, Jasper? Will you be leaving the Gulch also?"

"No, Millie. We have a snug cabin in the trees about two miles from here. We will be trying out some snowshoes which the reverend Dyer showed us how to make not too long ago."

"What is the purpose of snowshoes?" Asked Lucinda, brushing some snow from her shoulders.

"Well simply for walking on the top of the snow so as to keep from sinking into the depths. We'll head on over to the cabin first thing in the morning. Don't know how my burro Pepper will handle the deep snow. He's always contrary to new ideas. Any ideas, old or new, come to think of it."

"Snowshoes sound like an ingenious way to travel. We've had no misadventures today but it was arguably a struggle to make steady progress." Said Millie sticking her hands under the ends of her shawl.

"And how long would you, Otis and Pepper be staying at your cabin, Jasper? Not for the duration of the winter, surely. You doubtless would run short of supplies." Said Lucinda.

"We have been setting up stores for months since the late summer and fall. We have venison and rabbits frozen in a near-by ice cave. Think we'll be fixed quite nicely. I wish you could see the cabin, Lucinda. And of course you too, Miss Millie."

"Well, I can't envision that happening. It would hardly be proper. Even in this uncultivated Oro City. My word, we will freeze before long if we linger here much longer. Goodbye, Jasper."

"Yes. Goodbye Jasper. Please give my best regards to Otis, won't you?" Said Millie.

I prodded through the snow towards my burro's stall, whis-tling Otis' catchy tune, 'Ol' Susanny.'

Once there I began speaking aloud. "Now, I'm beginning to work on an idea, Pepper. It has to do with the object of my affec-tions. I have a notion to speak to Lucinda the very next time I see her. And just maybe she might be agreeable to me courting her in a more formal manner. And then, who knows?"

My burro snuffled and brayed.

The Finale

The town of Oro City - where fortunate placer miners picked up gold nuggets from the creeks and less fortunate men were driven by hopes of making a lucky strike – would never be a mark on Colorado State maps.

In time, the annoying heavy black sand, carbonate lead ore, was assayed - and found to have a high silver content. In the hills to the immediate north of California Gulch silver became the siren song. And for decades the hills streamed with tens of thousands of miners and their families. They say that those hills ran with silver. And Leadville was born.

But it was gold, not silver, which laid a solid foundation in that locale.

Jasper, Otis, Lucinda,Tom Starr, Augusta Tabor, and of course, Pepper typified the rugged, resilient, and well-intentioned individuals who inhabited a community known as Oro City. And on these pages their stories have been told.

ACKNOWLEDGMENTS

Personal interviews:

Father Leo Smith - February, 2018

Peter Donoher - March, 2018

Jim McEachern - April, 2018

John Yudnich - July, 2018

Additional thanks:

Max Ogden - Explaining blacksmithing & technical help.

Eli Jansen - Explaining blacksmithing.

Zoe Ogden - Reading early drafts & incomparable advice.

Noah Jansen - Formatting & technical help.

About the Author

Retired English teacher, currently lives in hometown of Leadville, CO, after decades elsewhere; loves grandkid visits, travel, and walks in the nearby hills.

Additional work by D.E. Vincent: CLIMAX kids, 1956

Lightning Source UK Ltd.
Milton Keynes UK
UKHW020643310521
384676UK00011B/974

9 781977 243096